CUPID BROKE MY HEART

LOVED FOR THE HOLIDAYS
BOOK ONE

ANNE STORM

Paperback Edition
ISBN: 979-8-89706-002-3

"IF MY STORY STARTED AT THE VERY BEGINNING, I WOULD TELL YOU how I got my name. Clea is unusual, for sure, and I have my mother to thank for that. She supposedly wanted to name me Cleopatra for who-knows-what reason, but she was so out of it that all she told the nurse was Clea before she decided it was a good time to take a nap." I took a sip of the whiskey sour that had been sitting in front of me before carrying on as if anyone really cared about my story.

"My mom didn't bother correcting that, and honestly, I'm sort of thankful. Cleopatra is a big name to live up to and I have enough problems. Starting with the day cupid screwed my life up. Yeah, the diaper wearing, bow-and-arrow carrying asshole who makes people fall in love. The bastard ruined my chance at finding my soulmate in college."

"How exactly did that happen?" The mystery man seated at the bar beside me asked.

"Well, sit back and relax because I have a crazy story to tell you…" I might have been three sheets to the wind already when I started this conversation with the heartthrob on the stool next to me. At least, I hoped he was actually a heartthrob and not a figment of my whiskey-goggled imagination.

"I was set up on a blind date…" I started my story.

⌇

Six Years Ago

"YOU HAVE TO GO!" Becs whined to me as she shoved another dress into my arms. "Here, try this, it'll be perfect!"

I groaned. My best friend in the world was only trying to help get me out before I stressed myself into an early grave. Becs had been my friend since we met in the third grade. There wasn't really a big story to tell about our friendship. She was the shy little girl with the unfortunate blonde bowl cut and the giant blue eyes

es. I was the girl with the honey-brown hair in lopsided pigtails with brown eyes and a smile that was too big for my face back then. We were awkward together in the best of ways, and for the most part, that never changed.

"A blind date? You want me to go on a blind date for Valentine's Day! What is wrong with you?"

"Nothing! It's not like you'll look desperate or anything. He doesn't have a date either."

My sigh should have made her back away, but instead, Becs just dug her heels in, or rather tossed me a pair of heels. I rolled my eyes. "There is no way I'm wearing heels."

"You have to. They go with the dress!"

"Do you remember the last time I wore heels?"

She thought about it so hard those cute little forehead wrinkles popped up right between her eyebrows. "I can't remember you ever wearing heels, now that I think about it." She paused for a moment while I tapped my foot impatiently. Then, I saw the moment it dawned on her because my best freaking friend in the world had the proper amount of second-hand embarrassment just from the memory that she cringed. "Prom," She finally said, somewhat reluctantly.

Becs snatched the shoes back. "Maybe, we'll just get you a cute little pair of kitten heels." Her mumbled plan only made me laugh.

"Or maybe this is a sign that I shouldn't go."

"I promise you that if you don't walk away from the night completely infatuated with the guy, I will never set you up on a blind date again!"

Intriguing notion. "Promise?" Becs nodded her head enthusiastically. "No, seriously, you have to pinky promise me, Becs."

"Fine," she stuck out her pinky and wrapped it around my own as we shook our hands together. "Pinky promise that if you are not completely infatuated with your date by the end of the night, I will never attempt to set you up again."

We were both twenty-one years old, but pinky promises were sacred business. I wasn't sure if that was scary or not. Becs thought of herself as a matchmaker, so for her to promise never to do it again, meant that she was overly confident I would hit it off with my blind date. Call me crazy, but that made me a bit giddy.

"Are you going to at least tell me about this guy?"

"Nope."

"Nope? That's all I get?"

Becs giggled. "I don't want to throw off any first impressions. I'll only tell you what he's wearing tonight. It will be something special because he needs you to notice him. As soon as we're done getting you dressed, I'll send a picture of you from the shoulders down, so he can recognize you too."

"Why not just a face shot? Seems like it would be easier."

"Because this is way more fun," she proclaimed.

"For whom?"

"Me, of course!"

Later, just before we arrived at the party, Becs leaned toward me and flipped her phone screen so that I could see it. She laughed at the shirt the man was wearing because it said: Cupid is a lying bastard.

"Well, I guess he's been burned before," I mentioned before laughing.

Becs shrugged. "Well, you both have that in common, otherwise you'd already have a date to this party."

"Ouch, Becs!" I laughed at my friend because she wasn't wrong. No matter what, the plan was to have a good damn night with or without Mr. anti-cupid.

"Did you send him a picture of me?"

"As soon as you get your ass out of the car, I will."

"Fine, let's do this!" I hopped out of the car, popped my hip out for a pose and grinned widely.

"You do remember there's no headshot in this picture, right?"

I nodded eagerly. "Yeah, that's why I'm not afraid to grin big. My stupid, crooked smile won't even show up."

"There's something wrong with you," Becs deadpanned. My answer was to point at the crooked smile I'd just talked about. She rolled her eyes, sent the text, and then took my hand and led me inside.

"Where is your date?"

"Inside already."

"Is it the Texas guy?"

She wiggled her eyebrows up and down. "Austin, and yes, it's him."

"Do you see that going somewhere serious?" I asked, curious, because Becs hadn't been interested in anything serious since we only had one year left of school. She'd been on several dates with the Austin guy though.

I was shocked when she shrugged her shoulders. "I really like him, so we'll see where it goes."

"That's a lot."

Instead of confronting the big change in her stance on dating, my best friend pulled me into the ridiculously sized Colonial house that served as the location of the party. It was some fraternity, and honestly, even after three years on campus, Greek culture was still a puzzle to me so I couldn't say for sure which frat house we stumbled into.

What I could say for sure was that there were bodies everywhere and I had somehow missed the theme of the evening. All the women were wearing red. I was the lone standout in a black dress. "Becs," I muttered as closely to her ear as I could get. "Did you forget something when you dressed me?"

She laughed. "Nope. I figured you would stand out more this way."

"I'm going to kill you. Dead. As in no longer breathing, Becs!"

"That's usually what dead means, dipshit!" She countered while tugging me in the direction of the makeshift bar in the corner. "First thing, we're getting you a drink to loosen you up," she insisted.

Just as we reached the bar, I saw him. The man wearing the Cupid is a Lying Bastard t-shirt. His face was hidden behind a balloon, but he was the only man wearing a black t-shirt with red letters on it. Those particular red letters. All the other men in the place were wearing white.

"Becs! I think I see him!" I yelled above the awful din of voices and bad techno music. I dropped my friend's hand and took one step in the direction of the man who was supposed to be my blind date, and then a diapered angel mowed me down.

No. That wasn't right. My startled eyes glanced up even as my body was falling, and there, above me without a care in the world was a giant fucking idiot dressed like cupid, complete with tiny white wings on his back, a diaper on his ass, and a fucking red bow and arrow set slung over his shoulder. The smug fucker didn't even realize…

"Oomph!" I cringed as my body hit a solid surface and hands

5

came around me. One grabbed my boob, the other my hip, before I was tugged up the body of a God.

"Are you okay?" He murmured in my ear. I spun, to get him to release the breast he still had hold of. "Oh shit! Sorry, I was just trying to catch you before your cute ass hit the floor."

I stared into hazel eyes that were surrounded by long, thick, dark lashes that I envied. His chiseled, clean shaven jawline made me want to run my hands across the skin there to see if it was as soft as it looked or as hard as his bone structure made it seem. His nose was long and straight and seemed to point straight to lips that were the tiniest bit too thin for my liking, but hey, if he was any more perfect, he really would be a God among men at this party.

"Thank you," I finally managed to say as Becs moved in close.

"Are you okay?"

"Yeah, I am now. Thanks to…" I left the sentence hanging, hoping my mystery savior would fill in the blank with his name.

"Jeff," he provided before reaching a hand out to my best friend. She stared at him as though he were the dirt beneath her cherished, red-soled heels.

"This is my best friend, Becs," I introduced since she didn't seem to care to.

"And that would make you?"

"Here on a date," Becs answered for me.

"Oh! The two of you are together?" Jeff asked, his eyes widened almost comically in surprise. I burst out laughing at his expense before slapping a hand playfully against his very firm pectoral muscles.

"No. I was supposed to meet a blind date here," I corrected.

"Oh, well his loss is my gain."

"Wait!" Becs yelled. "He didn't lose, he's here somewhere."

"No," Jeff said assuredly. "He lost because there's no way I'm letting this beautiful woman out of my sight now."

Becs huffed. "Do not go anywhere!" She threatened before

flouncing off, no doubt in a rush to go find my "Mr. Right" according to her.

All he ever was to me was blind date guy though. With Jeff standing there unable to take his gleaming eyes off me, after rescuing me from a potentially disastrous spill onto the sticky, frat house floor, I no longer cared about the blind date I was supposed to meet.

"We should probably get out of here and get to know one another before your friend comes charging back with the dude who she tried to set you up with," he suggested. When I just stared at him, he finished his thought. "I don't mind fighting for the lady of my dreams, but it might ruin your night and our chances to get to know one another."

Yeah, if I was wearing panties underneath this far-too-tight dress, they'd be soaked. Actually, I might need to snatch a napkin from the bar and find an inconspicuous way to keep from dripping down my thighs. I would honestly hate myself for that thought later, but it was a reality I had to contend with in the face of Mr. Too-fucking-handsome. My knight in… white cotton. It was only then that I realized he was only wearing what looked like white linen shorts and a white linen button up. Apparently, he had no problem adhering to the dress code.

2

SIX YEARS LATER

"ARE YOU JUST HAVING COLD FEET? YOU GUYS HAVE BEEN together so long."

"There's just something in my gut telling me things aren't right." I took a sip of my mimosa. Normally, day drinking wouldn't be something I'd do, but I was off work for the rest of the day. Unfortunately, I had plans of the wedding variety. It was time to go cake testing, and once again, Jeff couldn't be bothered to go with me for anything to do with our wedding, so I had to drag along my best friend.

"I know that it sounds like a case of cold feet and nothing more, but Jeff has been behaving oddly for the past few months. Hell," I huffed out a frustrated breath. "Maybe it's been more like a year now. After he finally proposed, everything went downhill. He's become distant, gone for work more than he's home, and then there are the trips. The ones he used to invite me on, if I had the time off or it was just a weekend jaunt. He hasn't even asked me to go on one in eight months, Becs."

"Maybe he's just nervous since the engagement and afraid things will change?"

I laughed. "Well, obviously they did change, and not for the better. But that was all on him."

She focused on me and really took in what I was saying then. "Do you think it's something more?"

"I think he's having an affair," I admitted.

She sat back and gasped. "Jeff wouldn't cheat on his 'Goddess of a Girlfriend'," she responded while using finger quotes exactly the way that Jeff would have done when saying that. I could hear the sarcasm dripping from her words. My best friend never did like Jeff. She would play devil's advocate with me all day, but in her mind, she probably already had him tried and convicted.

"I don't have any proof," I admitted. "Just this feeling."

"Honey, you know that I'm a gut-instinct kind of girl and my instincts have always said Jeff was a schmuck." She held her hands out, as if to stave off my argument. "I know, I'm biased because the man I set you up with the night you met Jeff is really who you're supposed to be with in life." We both chuckled because after six damn years, my best friend still insists that the set up was with my soulmate. I rolled my eyes as she continued. "The thing is, if you've been feeling it for months now, then you're probably not wrong. He'll try to make you think that you are though. But look," she held her arms up, indicating our surroundings. "He should be the one here, taking you to lunch, and going to the cake testing with you. It's his wedding too. Where is he?"

I bounced my shoulders up and down in defeat. "Supposedly, he's at work and couldn't get away." I looked at my phone to see if he had sent any messages telling me that he was able to get out of work and meet me at the bakery, but to my horror, I discovered that my phone wasn't in my purse.

"Shit! We need to run back to my office. I left my phone."

"All right, I'll get the check and we'll walk over really quick."

That was the good thing about our beautiful little town. It was just big enough to give that city feel without all the urban problems. We were on the cusp of blooming from small town status to something a little bit bigger and while I enjoyed the quiet of our small town, it couldn't hurt business to have a few more people and businesses in the area.

"Why is the light on?" I questioned out loud.

"You left it on?"

I shook my head. "No. I always turn it off when I leave."

"Maybe your prissy-pants assistant put something on your desk?"

Again, my head swiveled back and forth. "She's not allowed in my office when I'm out. She doesn't even have a key. Anything that is important for me goes in a special folder on her desk so I can just grab it whenever I get back in."

"Well shit," Becs muttered as I opened the door and realized that I was apparently wrong about my assistant not having a key somehow.

There was my assistant Hillary – the one who just informed me that she was three months pregnant – bent over my desk with a man slamming into her from behind. It was clear how she got pregnant, since the man also wasn't using protection.

"What in the hell are you doing in my office?" I shouted about the same time I noticed that Becs was standing beside me with her phone up, apparently recording the action. She shrugged when I gave her a questioning glance.

"It's for HR," Becs whispered. "In case she tries to lie."

I nodded and watched as the man was going to town behind my soon-to-be former assistant startled upon hearing my voice and turned just enough that I could see it was my fiancé, Jeff.

There really was no telling what came over me at the time, but my response was to laugh before I pointed to my assistant. "Is that *your* baby that my assistant informed me she was pregnant with earlier today?"

Jeff's eyes went comically wide as he asked, "What baby?" He seemed reluctant to take his eyes off me, but he turned to Hillary, as if to have her answer the question he just asked.

"I haven't told him yet," Hillary shouted at me, as if I were somehow the person in the wrong in this whole fucked up scenario.

"Seriously? You think me telling *my fiancé* about your baby news is the biggest problem here? It couldn't possibly be the fact that you've obviously been fucking my him for months, since you claimed you were already three months along earlier. Or, I don't know, maybe that you apparently broke into my office to fuck him here today, or the fact that you're both still showing off way more to us than we care to see?" Neither of them took the time to answer me as they scrambled to get their body parts back inside their clothing and make themselves presentable again. As if I could ever unsee everything that I just witnessed.

Once they had themselves relatively put together again, I nodded my head, as if a decision had just been made. Maybe it had. I was honestly in a fog and just winging this shit.

"Get the fuck out of my office!" I shouted at them when they simply stood there staring at me while I attempted to process everything. I turned cold eyes toward my assistant before either of them could comply. "And in case it wasn't already obvious, Hillary, you're fired!"

"W-what?" She stammered. "No! You can't! I'm pregnant. That would be discrimination."

"You were just caught fucking a man on my desk and you had to break into my office in order to do that. Never mind that the man in question *was* my fiancé, because breaking into my office is an offense worth firing you for all on its own. So is having sex in the workplace. This isn't a fucking brothel, and you weren't employed to whore yourself out here."

"I am still your fiancé," Jeff attempted to argue. I'm not sure why, or what he thought would come of his affair, but he had obviously lost his damn mind at some point if he thought I'd ever stay with him after this.

"Nope. Hillary is officially fired, and you are no longer anything to me beyond a sad story about my past."

"We have a life together," Jeff argued again.

"No," I corrected him. "We HAD a life together. We no longer do. Even if I were the type of woman to forgive cheating – and let's be clear, I'm not – I will not help you raise your mistress's baby!"

"I don't even know if it's mine."

"Considering you weren't wearing a condom when I walked in on you fucking her, and you weren't aware she was already pregnant, I'd say the chances are pretty good that you might have knocked her up at some point. And that reminds me, I need to schedule an appointment with my gyno to get tested for nasty diseases."

My bastard ex glanced down to where he'd hastily tucked his dick away and there was a noticeable wet spot there that made everyone in the room cringe, except Hillary, who was staring daggers at Jeff. It could have been because he claimed not to be the father or because he outright stated in front of her that it wasn't over between us. Either way, I didn't really care.

"Please, Clea," he begged. "My mom will kill me and worse, disinherit me, if she finds out I cheated on you."

"Maybe you should have thought about the consequences of sticking your dick where it didn't belong before you did it."

"We're in love!" Hillary chimed in unsolicited and clearly incensed that I claimed Jeff's dick didn't belong poking around inside of her.

"No! We are not!" Jeff snapped at his mistress. I almost felt bad for her, but truthfully, what did she expect when she was messing around with a man who had been in a supposed serious relationship for six fucking years with the woman he was engaged to. She couldn't have anticipated a happily ever after ending.

"But you said…"

"Only because you felt bad about fucking you when my fiancé didn't have time for me."

That was cold.

"You're disgusting!" I told Jeff. "Good luck with raising two children," I threw at Hillary, who pouted. "Now, get the hell out of my office before the police are called to remove you!"

Both scurried out of the office as I picked up the phone on my disheveled desk and dialed maintenance. "I need someone to come clean my office immediately."

"Ma'am, we schedule cleaners for after normal business hours."

"I understand that, but I also know there is always someone available from maintenance. I need my office cleaned, specifically my desk, and the person needs to use gloves when they do it. Also, the locks for my office door need to be changed immediately."

"Um, I'll have someone on that right away," the man in charge of our maintenance and security department barked into the phone. "Will that be all?"

"Oh, one more thing, I need security tapes from the hallway leading into my office, my assistant's desk, and anything from my office since I left at 11:15 this morning until now."

"Yes, ma'am." As soon as the words were out of his mouth, I hung up.

"You have cameras in here?"

"I do because you just never know."

"Aren't you worried about forgetting they're there?"

"No. I'm more worried about things going down and having the video to back me up, or catching people stealing from me. Remember my last assistant before Hillary? She was stealing money out of my purse when I went to the bathroom."

"That's crazy. Why would she do that?"

"Don't know, but when no one believed me, I had the cameras installed and we caught her red handed. She had also been stealing from my petty cash drawer, which she had access to so that she could grab stuff we needed for meetings or working lunches."

"I think maybe you need a male assistant next time. The last two have been bad luck."

"What I need is a robot assistant, right after I take the longest fucking vacation known to working man!"

Becs giggled, but quickly pulled a somber face before throwing her arms around me. "Seriously, are you okay?"

I hugged her back fiercely. "I guess I got my proof."

"Yeah, you sure did." She patted my back twice before letting go of me and stepping back. "Let's get your phone, cancel your appointment, and go get drunk while I get you set up with a doctor visit for this week."

"Strong drinks. Really. Fucking. Strong!" I insisted.

3

When my ex-assistant tried, and failed, to launch a workplace discrimination lawsuit against me for wrongful termination, word got out rather quickly about the small-town office scandal, the cheating fiancé, duplicitous pregnant assistant, and the poor working woman who not only had to deal with having her heart broken by an affair, but also had to have her reputation dented by the early accusations and lies from the other woman.

That was my life in a nutshell for the past four months, and it didn't even end there. Jeff's mother came over and helped me pack all of his shit up and get it out of the house we had shared. Luckily, the house was in my name only since it was willed to me two years earlier by my Great Aunt Melinda. She was nuttier than squirrel shit, but I always entertained her stories and made time for her, so I suppose her leaving me the house had been reward for not abandoning her altogether like most of the family had done.

"Have you seen the latest?"

I groaned as Becs made her way into my office after bypassing my new, nearly useless, assistant altogether. "What now?"

"There are three women claiming to be pregnant with his

baby. Two have shown proof of their pregnancies, and I guess they're all still pending a DNA test to show that the babies are actually his."

I sat with my jaw gaping open. "Are you kidding me?"

My best friend shook her head as somber eyes stared back at me. "Was your doctor absolutely certain you're in the clear?"

I bobbed my head emphatically. "I made him test me for everything and then some," I explained.

"And then some?"

"Well, while we were there, I told him to go ahead and run shit for strep throat, the flu, rabies, freaking Lyme disease, and anything else that asshole might have possibly passed on to me."

Becs nearly fell out of the chair she'd plopped down into. "Oh my God!" She wheezed amid her laughter. "Fucking rabies?" She sobered a bit. "Did he actually do that one?"

I shook my head. "He threatened to throw water on me. When I told him to do whatever it takes, he said I couldn't have rabies because just the threat of water touching me would have made me angry."

Becs was balled up in the chair laughing once more. "Oh shit, Clea, I think I just pissed in my panties a little bit."

A throat cleared from over by the doorway and I glanced up to see my assistant standing there with a man who couldn't hold back his own laughter. "Sorry, he said he had an appointment."

"Which is why Becs shouldn't have been allowed into the office, no matter how much she begged," I hinted so that my assistant would know we were going to discuss it later.

"Oh, she didn't beg. That woman just walked right past me like I wasn't even there." I sighed again, much to the man in the doorway's amusement.

"Austin?" Becs asked as the man moved in closer.

"Becs," he returned, though somewhat coolly.

"What are you doing here?" She asked, her voice sounding far away for a moment. It took me a little while to place the name with their history. He was "Mr. Texas", the guy I used to tease her about all the time before the fateful Valentine's Day blind date that never happened. I'd give it to Becs. The man was ridiculously handsome in that rugged way of lumberjacks. He had a full, dark beard and mustache, killer dark brown eyes that were nearly black in appearance and felt like they could see right into your soul even while simultaneously hiding his from view. There wasn't really a need to talk about his body, but if ever a fit, well-built lumberjack was going to wear a business suit, this man would be their poster child.

He held his hand out to me. "Austin Mercer, we had an appointment." I shook his hand before taking a seat in my own chair again while my best friend just sat there gaping at him. "It's good to know we're in the clear with your rabies test, but um, maybe this one needs to go have it done too?" He hitched his thumb toward Becs and that was finally enough to snap her out of her stupor.

"What?" She stood angrily. "Fuck you, Austin." It took only a second for her to remember where she was when her face burned bright red and she turned to me to apologize. "I'm so sorry, Clea. I didn't…"

I waved her apology off. This was not the time for it. "Becs, can you leave us so that we can get down to business and we'll talk later?"

"Sure. Yeah," she added as she backed toward the office door. "Sorry," she mouthed again once she got there, just before disappearing out into the hallway.

"I apologize-"

"No need," Mr. Mercer cut me off rather rudely before I could explain the presence of someone else here who also had no problem insulting my potential client. Well then, he was still here, so I would have to salvage the appointment by getting straight down to business.

"What can I do for you today?"

"I have a business that is in desperate need of a makeover."

"I think you might be mistaking what we do here," I tried to explain.

"The thing is, my brothers and I just bought a bar and it doesn't have the best reputation. What I want to do is hire some actors to come stage some good times at the bar, so we can air it in commercials and print ads."

"I see. Have you already made over the bar in the physical sense?"

The man before me nodded and in the process a few strands of his dark, otherwise slicked back hair fell across his forehead and dangerously close to his left eye.

"Okay, and what kind of campaigns are we looking at? About how many people do you think you'll need?"

"Ideally?" He asked the question and waited for me to nod my head in response before he carried on. "We'd like to make it look like there's a packed house. So, I guess however many you need for that."

"May I ask where this bar is located?"

"You remember Ned's Nest?"

I chuckled. "The old roadhouse with the boarded-up windows that doubled as a strip club when the law wasn't paying attention?"

"That would be the one."

I pressed my lips together in a tight line in an attempt to laugh at the unfortunate bar, but after a moment I managed to ask the all-important question. "What have you renamed it? Maybe we can start there."

"Tippler's Lounge."

I started to repeat it, brow furrowed as I thought about what it meant, and finally it dawned on me. I chuckled. "As in the drunkard's lounge?"

"Got it in one," he grinned as he confirmed the meaning.

"Oh my God! That is too perfect!"

"See, we're already off to a great start. Do you think you can help us get some shoots set up? We'll need some local faces in the mix too, since we want it to look believable."

"Of course," I agreed before glancing down at my calendar. "Can it be ready for an impromptu party in two weeks?"

"Yeah, why?"

"Valentine's Day. I think if you're willing to throw in a few free drinks for the participants, we can keep the budget fairly reasonable. You can either go with a lonely-hearts themed party or a lovers party, whichever you and your brothers prefer."

"Well, that's an easy one."

"Why is that?"

Austin stared at me for a moment and then shook off whatever he'd been thinking. "My brother and I both hate Valentine's Day, so we'll probably go with a "Fuck Cupid" theme."

"Yeah, I hate that asshole too," I muttered.

"What did Cupid ever do to you?" He asked.

I raised a brow, because there was no way in hell he'd missed all the drama surrounding me lately. "Well, he bumped into me at a party years ago, and that's how I met my ex-fiancé, the one who apparently has three, maybe four, babies on the way from just as many women. All of them conceived when we were together and planning our wedding."

I watched Mr. Mercer's eyes drop down my body, as if looking for evidence of one of those pregnancies. "I am not, nor have I ever been, pregnant. Thankfully."

"Well, congratulations on that, at least. Sorry that you had to go through everything you've been through though." He sat there thoughtful for a moment before turning those soul penetrating eyes on me once more. "Did you say you bumped into Cupid?"

"No. I said that Cupid bumped into me. Some frat guy dressed in a diaper, with a bow and arrow slung over his shoulder, mowed me down at a party years ago. My ex is the one who caught me before I hit the floor and we started dating after that."

"Huh," the man huffed.

"What does 'huh' mean?"

"Oh, nothing. Sorry. So, we're throwing a party and offering free booze to people in the hopes that they show up and agree to be on film?"

"Exactly." I grinned at him. "Sure does beat our normal modeling fee per person involved."

"I bet." He stood and reached out for my hand again. "Hammer out a contract and the contingencies, and I'll get a copy to my brothers so they can look it over too."

"Will all of you need to sign or do you have one person designated?"

"It'll just be me, but I like to make sure everything's good with them too before I add my signature."

The minute Austin Mercer let himself out of my office, my best friend found her way back in with a scowl on her face.

"What did that asshole want?"

"He wanted me to supply a party full of models and locals for an image rebuild at the bar he and his brothers purchased." If it was possible, Becs' scowl deepened.

"What happened with him anyway? You never did say."

"I didn't want you to think it was your fault," she tossed back with a wave of her hand as if I would just forget the whole thing.

"Um, no, we're not doing that," I told her. "You really need to tell me now."

"Your blind date was supposed to be his brother." I just stared at her, not understanding what the hell she was talking about. I hadn't been set up on a blind date in… Damn! It dawned on me then.

"The party where I met the asshole. The reason I hate Cupid!"

Becs chuckled. "You loved Cupid for years for that accidental fix-up."

"Well, I was stupid." I shrugged my shoulders as my friend

laughed at me again. "So, that guy who just walked out of my office was your boyfriend-"

"Friends with benefits is more like it," she interrupted to correct me.

"Okay, well I remember you wanting to be more than just that with him. He dumped you because I never met up with his brother at that party?"

"Saying that he dumped me would be putting it mildly." My eyebrows rose damn near into my hairline. There had been a lot my friend hadn't confided in me about back then, it seemed. Now, I had more guilt and more hatred for my ex. "He ghosted me completely."

"Yeah, I haven't talked to him since that night. When he saw you with someone else, he was angry, said that I'd promised not to screw his brother over if I set shit up because he wasn't in a healthy enough place to take it well." It was Becs turn to shrug her shoulders. "As if his brother's mental health was my responsibility or that I could control you, that dumbass diaper-wearing Cupid, or anything else that happened that night."

"Becs, I'm so sorry. You were so excited about your Texas guy."

"Nope! You're not putting his bullshit on your shoulders. He thought I was responsible and ghosted me for it, that's on him and no one else. As far as I see it, he did me a favor since his response was to bail and ghost me for things I couldn't control. Imagine if he got me pregnant and did that? Good riddance," she tacked on in the end as she dusted her hands together as if to clean off the memory of the man himself.

The man who had, at some point, found his way back to the doorway of my office. "Sorry," he mumbled, looking completely unlike the confident man that strode into my office earlier. "I think my phone slipped out of my pocket," he indicated the chair Becs was sitting in. Becs stood, glanced down, found the phone, and then left it there as she walked to the other side of my office to look out the window.

I don't know who I felt worse for as I watched their drama play out before me. Definitely my best friend, because my girl would always come first, but that didn't mean I missed the slumped shoulders, reddened ears, and overall embarrassed and sorrowful demeanor of Mr. Texas, also known as: Austin Mercer. It was clear that he heard every word of what Becs said and must have hated himself just a bit for a rash decision he made six years ago.

Welcome to the club, buddy!

"Thanks," he grumbled before turning abruptly, with his phone in his hand, and marching back out of my office without so much as a backward glance.

I jumped up, after he left and moved over to Becs. "You okay?" I whispered in her ear while offering a reassuring hug.

"That was only slightly embarrassing."

"More so for him."

She scoffed and turned to face me. "Yeah, right."

"Well, if you had seen him, you'd understand. His shoulders were hunched in like this," I slouched and made my shoulders come up damn near to my ears. "And the tips of his ears were red as freaking cherries."

That at least earned a tiny giggle from my bestie. "His ears only turn red like that when he's really embarrassed, so I guess you weren't lying to make me feel better."

"Nope. But I think you were lying to me, and maybe yourself, about how serious things were getting with him before he ghosted you."

"Doesn't matter. It's all in the past now."

I wasn't so sure about that, but I let it go because I still had work to do and a party to plan that people needed to be invited to.

4

Austin Mercer requested that I meet him at his bar so that he could sign the contract on both the party planning side and for the model release forms that would gain everyone entry to the anti-Valentine's Day party as well as two free drinks each.

He and his brothers had turned Ned's Nest into Tippler's Lounge in short order. The place looked more like a throwback to speakeasy bars of old rather than the slimy, backroom blowjob factory that Ned's Nest had been.

"Did you do away with the gloryhole in the bathrooms?" I asked as Austin greeted me.

He threw his head back and laughed as a blond version of him came strolling by. "Did you need a new job, sweetheart?" The asshole asked. It was only when I narrowed my eyes and really took notice of him that his familiarity struck a chord.

"You," I hummed the word out while lost in thought.

"So is that a yes or a no because honestly, we were just discussing whether or not to patch over the gloryhole." His smirk reminded me of something and suddenly, I had a flashback of a blond man in a diaper wearing a red bow and arrow strung over his shoulder.

"YOU!" I stared him down, throwing a little extra evil invective string of grumbled words along with it.

"What? Did I forget to call?"

"You're the reason I was engaged to the world's worst cheating asshole."

"How in the hell is that MY fault?" The blond version of Austin laughed as he asked the question. It only made me want to punch him in his smug face.

"You're Cupid!"

"What the fuck kind of crazy are you talking?"

Austin stepped in then. "Remember that frat party you crashed about six years ago?"

"The one where you dumped the girl of your dreams because of her stupid ass friend?"

Austin's ears reddened as he glared at his brother and tried hard to ignore me. "Yeah, you were dressed as cupid."

"Oh yeah! Man, I couldn't keep those bitches out of my fucking diaper. Never knew there were so many sorority girls with a weird "mommy" fetish."

"Oh God! I think I just threw up in my mouth a little," I admitted out loud after gagging.

"So, what does my costume have to do with your fucking bad choices in life partners?"

"Apparently, you knocked her over like an asshole, didn't apologize, and the dickwad who caught her took her from the party and started dating her."

"Oh," he shrugged as he said it as if those actions didn't matter in the least. "Too bad."

"Too fucking bad?" Austin raged at the man who I assumed was his brother. "You doing that ruined what I had with Becs AND you ruined Houston's blind date too."

"How the fuck do you figure I'm responsible for all of that?"

"That's what I'd like to know," a third man said from somewhere behind me. I turned to see another handsome man with short-cropped, dark-hair, a closely trimmed beard, gorgeous smile, and dark aviator glasses that hid his eyes from view.

"Houston, meet Clea. She was your blind date at that party." When everyone just gaped at Austin, he cleared up the confusion. "The one that you never got to meet that night because our dumbass brother here knocked her right into someone else's arms."

"Oh shit!" Blondie gasped before taking a few careful steps back from the two men who were openly scowling at him. "I had no clue."

"You never do," The man who had been identified as Houston grated out before turning and walking away from all of us.

"Maybe I should come back another time?" I asked.

"No, Dallas was just leaving," Austin told me before guiding us both to the bar. "Let's get this taken care of because we don't have much time to get things organized.

I couldn't help glancing back over my shoulder in the direction that Houston had gone. He was meant to have been my blind date that night? If I didn't want to punch Cupid in his junk before, I definitely did now. After standing the man up, on Valentine's Day no less, there was no way I'd ever get a second chance to make it up to him. Wasn't that just a shame?

"He won't be coming back out to join us," Austin said, drawing my attention back to him.

"Oh, I wasn't waiting for him to. Sorry, lost in thought."

"Regrets from that night?"

I laughed. "You heard my woe-is-me story the other day at the office, so you know I have all the regrets." I slipped the contracts out of my satchel and placed them down on the bar. "The thing about regrets is that they don't really do anyone a whole lot of good. So, instead, there's a win column and a loss column in life. You just have to hope that at the end of each day you have more wins than losses."

"What if you have more losses?"

"Then you work twice as hard the next day to change that."

"Sounds like good advice."

"Sure is, but I'll admit, I'm better at doling it out some days than acting on it."

Austin chuckled as he pulled the contracts close enough that he could read over them. "Do you at least learn a lesson from the rash decisions that lead to the losses?"

"Nah. Sometimes impulses bring us to the best places in our lives. My business was an impulse. Originally, I was going to run off to New York or Chicago and go try my hand at advertising and marketing for one of the big firms up there, but divine intervention held me back."

"Divine intervention?"

"My crazy aunt died and left me her house, so I couldn't pass up free housing. It made me realize we had a large enough community here that was growing and needed someone to help their businesses too. And when things were slow, I planned parties to get by."

"I was wondering how the two businesses collided like that. It works out better for me, so I'm not complaining."

"I'll be sure to tell my aunt you said 'thank you' next time I talk with her."

"Um," He hummed out, eyeing me suspiciously so I went with it.

"Yeah, she reincarnated into my cat. Swear that woman just refused to give up that house completely."

"Your cat?"

I nodded emphatically. "Yeah. Don't worry, Aunt Melinda is fully litter box trained and everything."

"You're a gullible sap," someone mentioned, and once again the stealthy brother was standing there laughing at Austin. I joined in.

"He really bought it for a minute there."

"It could have worked to your benefit if you'd told him that she sprayed your favorite pair of shoes. That kind of little gross detail really sells the story."

"Well, thank you, sir, for aiding my future lies."

"My pleasure," Houston mumbled before snatching up the contracts that were sitting in front of his brother, who was just gaping at us. "This is both the party planning and the photography release?"

"Yes, the bottom stack are the photography release forms. Everyone who enters will need to fill one out, including any staff you have. No photo release, no entry because we won't want to take the time to track down people who didn't want to be in the pictures so that they can be photoshopped out of the frames."

"Gotcha." He took a closer look at both then handed them back to his brother. "I approve. Get everything set up," and just like that he turned and left again. The man was a bit of an enigma, but I wasn't sure that I was able to solve that particular puzzle.

Austin started signing the paperwork and turned to me with a grin. "Don't mind him. He's been broody like that for years."

"Why?"

"You know how your ex-fiancé was running around getting women pregnant while you were planning your wedding?"

I nod, because what else can I do?

"Well, in college, my brother proposed to his girlfriend only to find out she was pregnant with his best friend's baby. She broke down and confessed while he was kneeling there in the middle of the quad."

I had heard about that during my junior year. "Oh no! That was your brother?"

"Yep, and the first time he agreed to date someone after that was the blind date that Becs and I set you two up on."

"Oh shit!" Hy heart stumbled inside my chest.

"Yeah, it did nothing for his confidence back then. It's a good thing he didn't know it was our own bonehead brother who ended up throwing a wrench in the works."

"Well, he does now."

"He's in a better place now." Austin tried to sound convincing, but something about it didn't ring true.

5

"ARE YOU SURE IT'S OKAY IF I'M THERE?"

"I'm allowed to bring a plus one and no one said that it couldn't be you, so yeah, I'm sure." I stuck my tongue out at my bestie as she worried over her hair once more. Her dark hair curled down her back in chunky spirals that I wished I could get my hair to do. Unfortunately, mine would never hold curls. The best I could do was add some warm honey highlights to my light brown hair and then hope for the best whenever I tried to style it in anything other than the way it normally hung mostly straight down my back.

"You can be so difficult."

"I know you're trying to be supportive, but honestly, if seeing him again is going to bother you then you don't have to be there."

"No, I want to," she whined. "He's just... he hurt me," she admitted in a small voice. "When he just ghosted out on me, it was worse than a breakup because I was left not knowing what in the world happened."

"Do you think it would help you to know?"

"No. I kind of got the picture already. He was angry with me because of you running off with someone else instead of going on that date with his brother. And, as luck would have it, it was their younger brother who unintentionally screwed it all up for everyone." She rolled her eyes. "Bet he didn't ghost his brother over that when he found out."

I laughed. "Can you imagine?" A fine shimmer of gloss coated my lips as I stared into the mirror wondering if maybe I should wear a different shirt. I pulled at the hemline once more and Becs slapped my hand.

"Leave it. I think the shirt is perfect."

I glanced at the shirt Becs had specially made for me this year. It had a cartoon woman punching cupid in the diaper region and below that it said: Cupid is a lying bastard.

Yup. Just like the shirt my blind date had been wearing the night I accidentally stood him up. Granted, the cartoon violence made it even better.

The bar that the Mercer brothers owned wasn't that far from my house, so once we were ready, we took off so that we could get there early and make sure the staff had everything set up and ready for guests to arrive. What neither of us were expecting was the line of people already waiting outside to be allowed in.

"Wow! I guess everyone hates Cupid as much as you do." Becs laughed as we passed them all by and parked in the employee section of the lot.

"I guess so. I think this is a better turnout than we had hoped for. It seems like word of mouth spread and maybe we better get someone out here with a clipboard and have people pre-sign their photo release forms."

"You're the boss!"

"No, Becs, your Texas guys are the boss. I'm just here to help them out tonight.

"I prefer to think of you as the boss," she argued. "It makes it easier to go into a place that belongs to him."

"You don't have to be here," I reminded her for the fiftieth time.

"Hush, come on, I hear this place is giving away free drinks tonight."

It took a minute for someone to come let us in the backdoor. Luckily, it was Jordan Pierson, one of the bartenders who signed on to work in this place, because I had met her when I came to drop off some of the party supplies.

"Hey! Come on in, Clea. I'm pretty sure we have everything set up, but I'm guessing that you want to double-check before they start letting bodies through the door." She grinned, already knowing me so well.

"Did you see the line outside?" I asked and Jordan shook her head. "Well, I hope you're ready because it is already wrapping around the block and that's something I never thought I'd see, let alone on an opening night."

Her eyes widened. "Do you think we should call for reinforcements? They only have me, Dallas, and two other bartenders on tonight."

"If need be, I'll hop in and help too," I informed her. I wasn't the greatest behind the bar, but I could sling beer with the best of them. "You do your mixologist thing and I'll hand out the beer."

Jordan's smirk let me know she understood exactly what my skill level was. Pretty much nonexistent, but I'd do whatever it took to make this night a success. It was my reputation on the line too, after all. If everyone saw that I was responsible for relaunching Ned's Nasty Nest into something as wonderful as the Tippler's Lounge, then word of mouth would spread, and hopefully more than my party planning side of the business would start blooming. My photographers were on hand tonight, along with a videographer, to capture the night in the best light possible.

"Where are your bosses?" Becs asked Jordan. A look passed between the two women that made even me squirm, though I had no clue what that was about.

"They're in the office going over some staffing stuff," Jordan answered before walking away. "Feel free to find me if you need anything, Clea." She called out as she moved away from us. I noticed that the same offer was not extended to Becs.

"What was that about?"

Becs sighed. "They used to date."

"Who used to date?"

"Austin and Jordan. They dated before he started seeing me back then."

"Before or during?"

Becs shrugged, but judging from the guilty look on her face, I was guessing that there was a bit of overlap in what went on between the two women and Austin. "Maybe one day, when I'm at the bottom of a bottle of tequila, I'll tell you all about it."

I scrunched up my nose.

"You don't drink tequila because of that one night."

"Exactly."

In other words, I'd never know what really happened between the three of them. All sorts of crazy love triangle scenarios were brewing in my mind as I walked, which was why I failed to see an obstacle in my way and instead tripped over it. My feet flew out from underneath me, and I prayed as I was going down that God at least spare my teeth. A black eye could heal. Fake teeth would suck.

"Whoa there," a deep voice soothed as a pair of very sturdy, muscled arms wrapped around my middle and pulled me back to standing. I was so grateful for the save, that I took a moment to lean back into the solid body that held me, smelling his subtle aftershave that tingled my senses and made me want to turn and bury my nose in the crook of his neck. When I finally managed to get my heart beating normally again, I turned in his arms, still afraid to let go of the contact, and found myself face-to-chest with Houston Mercer.

"Sorry, I tried to get to it before my brother could wreak havoc again, but..." I was puzzled for two solid minutes as I stared at him, until I realized he was pointing at something. When I glanced down, it was to see a red bow and arrow lying on the floor.

"Fucking Cupid!" I hissed while glaring at the offending equipment.

Houston's chest rumbled. "That's why I took him to the back room to beat his ass. I can't believe he planned to run around here in that same fucking getup that screwed everything up last time."

"I'm sorry." The apology was out of my mouth before I could pull it back.

"You don't have anything to be sorry for. We didn't know one another then, hadn't even met yet."

"Still, I knew you were there waiting for me. I just didn't think about it again after almost eating the floor in that nasty frat house."

"Well, someone else beat me to you that night. Too bad for him, he turned out to be a fucking idiot."

I laughed at that. "You could say that again."

"I could, but that would mean giving the asshole too much of our time, when he already had more than he ever deserved."

Oh, dear lord, apparently swooning was something women still did because my legs failed me, my heart fluttered uncontrollably, and I thought maybe just maybe I should ask if I can have this man's babies.

"I see you found my date for the night!" A snotty feminine voice called out from somewhere too close to be a coincidence. I turned my head at the same time Houston did. A move that would have had us standing cheek to cheek, if only he hadn't been about five inches taller than me.

"Samantha," he stated rather coolly.

Her eyes rounded out in mock surprise, the evil smirk gave her away though, as did the overly dramatic way she popped her hip out to the side. This woman was all attitude, and it was entirely directed at me since I was still wrapped up in Houston's arms. He must have realized it at the same moment I did because he gently set me back on my feet and took a hasty step back from me.

"This is Clea, she's the one helping us with the party, the advertising, and cleaning up the bar's past image." It was all said so business-like that I nearly turned to make sure it was still Houston standing at my back. Maybe this woman had good reason to give me the nasty glare that was still directed my way.

"Well, I'm pretty sure that pawing all over the owners of the bar is not in the job description, so I think you're done here." The woman stared me down as she spoke in a dismissive tone. One thing about going through a disgusting breakup with a cheater had taught me was not to cower in the face of bitchiness.

"Houston was kind enough to keep me from falling after I tripped over Dallas's toys. Whatever more you made of that scene in your head is your problem, not mine, but make no mistake, I won't tolerate your bitchy attitude toward me when I've done nothing wrong."

She huffed and then turned from me to Houston with a put-upon wounded look in her eyes and her mouth turned down in a pout. "Are you going to let her talk to me like that? I think she should be fired, right now!"

I didn't expect Houston to take my side and I planned on telling him that he would still be billed for the night, when he pulled me back into his embrace and kept an arm wrapped around my middle. To say the action stunned me would have been an understatement.

"Samantha, I invited you here as a friend and because you work for me, nothing more. That doesn't give you a license to come here and cause trouble, pretending there's something between us, and ordering me to fire the woman who put this whole night together for my brothers and me. You had the opportunity to step up and help with this place, and you said you were too busy and that it was a lost cause, if I recall correctly."

"I didn't realize you guys were serious about this place then." Her pout was still grating on my nerves because there was nothing genuine about it.

"Sam," he growled, as his arms tightened a little more around my midsection. I honestly wasn't sure if he was holding on to protect me, or if he was using me as a human shield.

"Houston!" She stomped her foot. "You invited me here. I assumed it was so that we would finally get together after you've made me chase after you endlessly for years. What I did in the past shouldn't matter anymore. You know things changed for me, and I expected you to-"

He laughed as he cut off her tirade. "You expected me to what, Sam? Was I supposed to wait around until you got done playing house with my cousin? You know - the man I once considered my best friend. The only reason it's over between the two of you is because he found out that he's not the father of that baby you had."

"It might be yours."

"If you thought for a second that the baby was mine, you would have never claimed it was his." I could feel the animosity pouring from the man at my back. "You might have conveniently forgotten, Sam, but I know what you did. I know how you got him into bed with you, and what your plan was. It didn't work because you expected me back sooner. I tried to be cordial with you as a way to keep the peace within the family. Since the baby you had isn't actually family, that's not really necessary any longer."

"What? You're just going to turn your back on me like that? We were in love!" Her voice carried to everyone else in the room, and it was the first time I realized that we had an audience watching. Granted, it was just staff – both mine and Houston's, his siblings, and Becs. They were all gaping at the scene that we made though. I kind of wished the floor would open and swallow me whole, considering I was still the monkey in the middle of this little war they had brewing. Quite frankly, I was growing nervous that either the she-bitch would shank me, or Houston would use my body as a weapon instead of just a shield.

"Swear to God, I'm never leaving home on Valentine's Day again," I mumbled under my breath, but Houston must have heard because I felt the rumble in his chest from his laughter.

"You're laughing at me?" Samantha asked, her eyes would have killed me if she could have done so with just a look.

"Nope. I'm done with you. I'm laughing at my date for the night."

"Your date?" Samantha groused, sounding almost as dumbfounded as I felt.

"Your date?" I managed to ask while tipping my head back to see his reaction.

Houston grinned down at me. "I seem to recall being stood up by my blind date on this day six years ago. You owe me."

"Well, we're off to a fabulous start. The only thing that could make this more awkward is if my ex came bounding in with all the women who he managed to get pregnant while we were together."

"We kind of have that in common." I gave him a dubious look that made him laugh while expounding on the idea. "See, we both have exes who made babies with someone else while we were supposed to have been together. I think that puts both of us firmly in the category of people who would never do that to someone else, which makes us perfect for one another, if you think about it."

"The fact that we both attract cheating degenerates makes us perfect for one another?" I deadpanned.

"Yeah, it really does. You'll see." He leaned in, kissed the top of my head, and then handed me off to someone else. I glanced around in time to notice it was Becs that he handed me off to. "I need to go put this shit away before someone gets hurt," he proclaimed as he lifted the red bow and arrow from the ground.

"We're not done here!" Samantha yelled at Houston.

"We've been done for years," he answered back as he continued walking.

"We work together," she argued again.

"If you don't want that to change, then I suggest you get your shit together and stop this." He groaned and then looked around for anyone else who would be willing to take on his headache. "Someone get her out of here and make sure she doesn't come back tonight."

"Gladly!" I realized it was Jordan and Austin who both spoke at once. When they grinned at one another, I glanced back at my best friend once more to see the frown on her face. I wished that she hadn't come to support me tonight, because it looked like it was going to cost her in ways she hadn't even fathomed before we left for the night. Her biggest concern before was seeing her ex again. Seeing him with the woman on the other tip of their triangle probably stung in bigger ways.

Houston turned to me, the tips of his ears reddening a bit in embarrassment over the situation. "Sorry about that," he murmured.

"None of that was on you," I informed him. "You're not responsible for other people's crazy."

He grinned back at me then. "Where were you when I needed to hear that years ago?"

"Falling into my own cesspool of crazy," I joked. It was weird to think that I was already in a place where joking about my failed relationship with my ex-fiancé was something I could do without sinking into despair.

"Come on!" It was an invitation and Houston held his empty hand out to me while still holding the damn bow and quiver full of arrows in his other hand.

Oddly enough, I didn't even question where we were going. I

just tucked my much smaller hand into his and followed him to the back of the bar. I assumed Becs would be hot on my heels to avoid being left behind with Jordan or Austin. To my surprise, when I glanced back, she stood there at the bar with a drink in her hands and a lost look on her face.

I stopped mid-step and when Houston's hold on me tugged, he turned to see what I was looking at and sighed. "I told him not to drop her just because things didn't work out with us," he admitted.

I shrugged. "What's done is done, but maybe I shouldn't leave her alone." Just as I said that, my videographer, Cory, sauntered over to Becs and started flirting hard enough that even my sad best friend cracked a smile.

"She'll be fine for a few minutes," Houston told me as he gave another gentle tug on our connected hands. I turned back and continued following him into the back hallway where the offices were located. Unfortunately for the both of us, we had the worst Valentine's Day luck ever.

"Oh God! It's everywhere, Dallas," a woman whined.

"Not for long," he cooed at her while gently pushing the woman to her knees in front of him.

"What in the absolute fuck are you doing?" Houston growled.

Instead of simply answering from his current position, Dallas startled and jumped a bit. In doing so, he also turned toward the direction of his brother's voice, so we both got a good look at what exactly was everywhere. Dallas stood there with his cock out, chocolate sauce dripping off the damned thing, and a bottle of Hershey's syrup in his hand. The startled expression quickly morphed into a grin as he caught sight of the bow and arrows Houston had in a death grip.

"Ah shit, I forgot to get rid of that," he laughed while speaking, but also turned toward the woman who was still kneeling in front of him. "Come on, honey, it's not gonna lick itself."

I groaned. Dallas was officially my least favorite Mercer brother.

"Dallas!" Houston's raised voice didn't seem to faze his brother as he guided the woman's head to his crotch. Jesus, she was really going to go for it in front of us. "Dallas, you stupid fuck!" Houston growled before gripping onto his brother's shoulder and yanking him back a step.

I had to turn my head to try to keep from laughing at the sloppy, chocolatey sight before me. The woman, who was still on her knees and finally looking a bit shell-shocked, had chocolate sauce all over her mouth, cheeks, nose, and chin. Her eyes were comically wide as she stared at the rest of the Hershey mess left behind on Dallas's rapidly deflating cock.

"What the fuck, Houston?"

"That's my line, you dipshit! This is opening night. After the shit that used to go down here, we were already warned someone might do a walkthrough of the place while we're open. Or did you forget that since you don't pay attention during our little meetings?" Dallas actually seemed to hear his brother that time. "This kind of shit, right here, will get us shut down before we even get to let the first fucking person through the fucking doors."

Dallas ran a hand haphazardly through his hair, trailing a bit of chocolate along the way as he did. Houston shook his head disapprovingly at his brother.

"I wasn't thinking," the younger Mercer admitted.

"That was obvious," Houston shot back. "Go get yourself cleaned up and take your friend with you."

"I'll be back," Dallas said as he held a hand out to help the chocolate-faced girl up off the floor.

"Don't bother. We needed you to be fucking serious for once, man. If you can't do that, then maybe you need to just be a silent partner."

"Shit, Houston!" Dallas muttered as he guided his girl of the night out the back door after leaving the bottle of chocolate on the counter. Houston grabbed a paper towel and wrapped it around the bottle before tossing it in the trash.

"That was most likely from inventory," he mumbled, more as a reminder to himself to make sure it was notated somewhere than to inform me.

"Is he always like that?" I asked.

"Irresponsible and childish?" He questioned. "Yeah. That has never changed. Dallas, being the youngest and the most spoiled, is our resident good-time sibling. He has never known a bad day in his life."

While I understood the sentiment, I had a feeling that Houston had his little brother pegged all wrong, but it wasn't my place to let him in on that secret. I had a good feeling that Dallas's behavior was a method to hide his own hurts.

"Well, shit," Houston turned to look at me as the words left his mouth. A smile bloomed on mine in return.

"I'll say this for us, things sure do get interesting when we're in the same building together."

The sparkle in his eyes returned, something I was grateful to see. "I'm beginning to think that's an understatement." He held up the bow and turned once more. "Let me lock this in the office and we can head back out to the main floor to check on things."

"Okay."

"Clea?" My name was a question on his lips.

"Yeah?"

"I don't want this to be all there is between us tonight."

"I just swore off men not too long ago," I told him. His face fell and that sparkle in his eyes dimmed again. I couldn't take seeing that, so I grabbed hold of his hand once more. "But there's no way I'd leave here tonight without making an exception for you."

"Just for me?"

"Only for you," I agreed. "As you said, we both know what it's like to be on the shit end of the stick in a relationship. If ever there was a person to put my faith in again, I'd like to think it would be someone who understands that whole-heartedly and never wants to do that to another person."

Houston didn't answer in words. Instead, he let go of my hand, reached out to wrap it around the back of my neck and pull me closer to him. His lips met my own before I could even register what was happening. Oh, dear lord, this man's lips had me wanting to climb him like a tree, or better yet, test out Dallas's chocolate sauce ideas. Maybe another time.

"Come on," Houston managed to say as our lips parted. "Let's get through tonight so that I can show you I mean business."

6

When we got back to the main part of the bar, the doors had already been opened and there were plenty of people ordering drinks, checking the place out, and enjoying the music. If Houston's face was anything to go by, I'd say he was proud of the turnout and everyone's early reactions. As well he should have been.

"I need to go make the rounds," he told me almost apologetically.

"Go, do your job. I have to check in with my photographers and videographers too."

Houston nodded. "Don't leave without us speaking again," he insisted. My head bobbed in acknowledgment because there was no way I would let that opportunity pass me up again. It's funny because just a day ago, I would have said that I never wanted to date again. At the very least, it would be a long time before I jumped back into the deep end of the dating pool. Somehow, Houston pointing out that we had both suffered at the hands of careless exes had calmed my urge to run as fast as humanly possible from any sign of love, lust, or even close friendship with the opposite sex.

"Hey," Becs startled me with that one word, and I turned to see she had walked up beside me.

"Hey."

"You have that look in your eye," she commented while her eyes stayed trained on the crowd.

"What look would that be?"

"The one where you can't take your eyes off a certain Mercer brother."

"Am I an idiot for even thinking of going there this soon?"

Becs grabbed my arm and spun me around. "The only idiot was your ex. You are a catch and I hate that you're second guessing your own possible happiness because he blew it." A funny look came over her face before she continued. "I guess maybe he got blown and that was the problem," she corrected.

"If that was the problem, he wouldn't have so many baby mommas lining up for paternity tests," I joked.

"Yeah, you're ready for this," she hummed out while still refusing to make eye contact.

"What makes you say that?"

"You can joke about what that asshole did without falling to pieces. That means you'll be fine."

We both stood there for a few more minutes watching the crowd. Okay – my focus was on a certain someone in the midst of all the partygoers. I wasn't sure exactly what my bestie was keeping her eye on. She kept bouncing back and forth between two spots. It looked like maybe she was watching Austin and Jordan. The pair were working opposite ends of the bar.

"You ever going to fill me in on what happened there?" I asked.

"Oh, look, isn't that your videographer trying to flag you down?"

I rolled my eyes and walked off because she wasn't wrong and I knew even though the man was trying to get my attention, it was also obvious that my friend did not want to talk about her past involving Jordan and Austin. I couldn't really blame her. Emotions had been involved, so it couldn't be easy to process seeing them together after she had been ghosted. It also wasn't easy to know that I was the reason behind her being ghosted. Suddenly, I felt like I owed my best friend more than I could ever repay her.

"What's up, Cory?"

The man took hold of my shoulders, spun me around, and then pointed over my right side to a balcony area that didn't seem to have an access point from the main bar area. "How can I get up there?"

"Um, I'm not sure, but we can go ask someone."

As it turned out, we didn't have to go ask anyone.

"Why are you manhandling your boss?" Houston grumbled, the low bass of his voice having no problem being heard over the music.

Cory didn't even miss a beat, as if the threat in Houston's tone had never been implied. "I need to get up to that balcony, so that I can get some shots of the whole crowd. Can you get me up there?"

"Yeah, I can. Follow me," Houston demanded, but he latched onto my hand with his own and tugged me along behind him too.

I hid the grin that threatened to explode on my face as we walked toward the hallway that led to the offices and stockroom.

"I don't remember there being a balcony there before."

Houston turned his head long enough to give me a raised eyebrow and a smirk. "Frequent visitor of Ned's Nest, huh?"

"Shut up!" I squealed while laughing off his taunt. "No, I checked the place out online when the listing went up because I thought it might make a great studio space and event rental."

"It was walled off with one-way glass when Ned owned the place. The perv used to sit up there and watch what went down. The balcony actually looks down over the dance floor and on the other side, it looked down on two of the," he coughed purposefully, "offices that used to be part of the backroom experience."

"Oh wow! I wonder how many people knew about that prior to Ned's departure?"

"I think that might have been the reason for Ned's departure. The old coot was blackmailing a good few people in our humble town from what I hear."

I couldn't help the laughter that bubbled up. "Well, good for him. You can't enter a den of sin and expect you're going to come out clean on the other side."

"Pretty sure that's what old Ned was banking on." We turned a corner and sure enough, there was a narrow set of stairs that curved up and around to a balcony on this side too. Truthfully, I should have noticed it earlier when we were back here, but chocolate covered dick trumps oddly placed stairs every time, I supposed.

"Can we go up?"

"We can," Houston said as he led the way. Cory followed but turned to waggle his eyebrows at me suggestively.

"Keep the filming classy, Cory," I reminded him.

"How did I know you'd take the fun out of it, Ms. Kincaid."

I grumbled a few expletives under my breath at my videographer's formal use of my last name. He only did it when he was amused with me because it chapped my ass to be seen as his elder.

There were still two and a half years between me and thirty, dammit. Cory was five years younger though, and he never let me forget it. Granted, that had a little something to do with the crush he once had on me. I ended up having to explain that I was seeing Jeff back when his crush first manifested. Then again, I made it clear that even if I hadn't been attached already, I wasn't a cradle robber, and Cory backed off aside from the silly little flirtations now and again.

"Wow!" I murmured, forgetting all about Cory and his silly

jokes as the view stunned me. It was definitely a different perspective to see all the lighting rigs in place that hung from the rafters. As I moved closer to the dance floor side, it quickly became clear why Cory had asked about getting up here. This viewpoint was going to be video gold. As if to emphasize my thought, Cory immediately started filming while Houston and I stood back and just took it all in for a few minutes.

"I can't thank you enough for all of this," he said, and I could feel his breath tease across the shell of my ear. The full-body shudder I gave in response made him chuckle. "Good to know that I can cause that kind of response in you too."

Too? As in, I had the same effect on him?

"I have to get back out there. Did you want to stay?"

I turned to Houston. "No, I need to be out there too." He put his hand out, palm upturned, waiting for me to join mine with his. There was no hesitation on my part until something out of the corner of my eye caught my attention. I spun toward the loud-ass Hawaiian shirt that I caught in my peripheral vision and nearly lost it enough to vault over the railing and go after the jackass for daring to be at one of my events.

"That son of a bitch!" I yelled. Houston stepped closer and glanced down. His quick grunt made it clear he knew exactly who that was.

"Come on, I'll have him escorted out once we get back down there."

I nodded but stopped beside Cory. "I better not see any part of him in any of the footage from tonight."

"Not a fucking chance," Cory agreed.

Houston was just putting his phone away after shooting a text off to someone when he took my hand and led me back to the stairwell that would take us out to confront my shady ass ex-fiancé. I couldn't believe the bastard was out partying, on Valentine's Day no less, when he had several women running around town pregnant with his babies.

For a solitary blip in time, I allowed myself to wonder once again, how in the hell I had missed it. What had changed? Was it just the impending marriage that sent him off the rails? Had he always been like this, and I hadn't seen it? I didn't think so, but then again, how was it possible for him to do a complete one-eighty in personality?

I didn't even realize we stopped walking, just at the door that would lead us back out to the main bar area, until Houston tugged at my hand that was still ensconced in his.

"Don't do that."

"Do what?" I asked.

"I can see the questions that are playing out in your mind right now. I know, because I've been there. Stop. His behavior isn't on you. If he'd been an adult about things, he would have come to you with his problems before he ever stepped out. He didn't. You didn't see it because it wasn't there before and because no one had given you reason to see something like that coming. I can promise you, that is something you will never have to worry about with me."

I nodded my head because if I tried giving a verbal agreement, I'd probably lose my battle with the tears. I wasn't crying over my ex, but the fact that someone saw inside me and understood the turmoil there.

"Okay, let's go throw out the trash, then we can get back to work." Houston winked and then guided us both out to where we had last seen Jeff.

The minute he spotted me, Jeff's eyes lit up. Then they traveled down and the pure joy that had been there moments ago diminished as he saw my hand wrapped in another man's.

"Clea?" The way my name formed a question sounded almost like an accusation.

"Jeff, what in the hell are you doing here?"

"I came to…" he stopped and took a harder look at Houston then. "I know you," he practically growled. "You're the asshole who was supposed to meet up with my Clea at that party where we met."

It was weird that he knew that considering I hadn't known who Houston was back then and had only seen the briefest glimpse of him before Jeff stepped in to catch me.

"Yeah, and you're the asshole who stood in my way then. Thanks for finally fucking up."

Um. What?

"Clea, this guy is a stalker!" Jeff accused.

"Says the serial cheating scum with several babies on the way by just as many women," I argued.

"I'm serious, Clea."

"So am I, Jeff. If you think I'd believe a word out of your treacherous, lying mouth, you have another think coming."

"We can talk about this and work through it, Clea. I just had cold feet."

"Yeah, Jeff?" I asked, feigning my curiosity. "You don't look like you're trying that hard to get me back while out partying on Valentine's Day."

"You're out too!" He declared.

"I'm working," I countered.

His eyes slid down to where my hand was still being held by Houston's. "Somehow, that doesn't look like work."

I bobbed my shoulders up and down indifferently. "I happen to like who I'm working with," I taunted.

Houston chuckled and then pulled me close to him as the men who were working security that night approached us. He inclined his head toward Jeff and the two burly security men moved in so that they could take the trash out without issue.

"What the fuck?" Jeff asked. "I haven't done anything."

"Really? Could have fooled me. Oh, wait, you did fool me. Right up until I walked in on you fucking your assistant. You know, the one who is pregnant with your baby. The one who says you were together for months. That's not cold feet, Jeff. That's duplicity. That's cheating. That's called 'never again' in my book. Enjoy all that child support you're about to have to pay out. Actually, maybe we should let you stay tonight. I have a feeling you won't be getting out much in a few months when all those baby bills come due."

"Oh shit!" One of the bouncers exclaimed. "This is *that* guy?" Both bouncers started laughing then. The one with his hand wrapped snugly around Jeff's bicep glanced back and forth between me and my ex. "You gave her up?" He asked.

"Must be stupid," the other bouncer said.

"Obviously, he has how many women knocked up now? Four? Five?" They both laughed again. "Come on, man, let's get you out of here before you stupidly add a sixth to the mix. Don't you know about condoms?" The bouncer asked as they escorted a very somber Jeff toward the front of the club.

"You okay?" Houston leaned down to ask.

I turned in his embrace and stared up into his soulful eyes. "Surprisingly, I am."

The smile that bloomed on Houston's face made me want to take him home and lock him up at my place where no one else would ever be able to see that smile but me.

"We might be able to work something out there," he chuckled as my face went from the picture of serenity over my wayward crazy thought to one of absolute confusion. He leaned in closer and whispered in my ear, "You said that part about locking me up in your house out loud. Glad you like my smile though." While I stood there in shock, Houston planted a kiss on my cheek, and then sauntered away like that didn't just happen.

Well, shit.

7

He asked me to wait for him, so I did.

"I think you're going to be really happy with these pictures," Sam was saying as he and Cory packed away all of their equipment.

"The stuff I shot from the balcony is going to be epic," Cory agreed.

"I can't wait to see how you both put it all together," I encouraged my team. They had never let me down in the past and I didn't expect that would change at all.

"Do you need a ride home?" Cory asked as he hauled his equipment bag up to his shoulder.

"No, I drove here with Becs."

"Okay, well, see you on Monday then." If I didn't know any better, I'd swear that he was pouting. Considering the grin Sam gave me before running off his buddy, I'd guess that was accurate.

"Looks like someone has a crush," Dallas teased. I hadn't even heard the evil, younger Mercer brother approach.

"Weren't you supposed to be knee-deep in chocolate sauce somewhere?"

Dallas grinned widely. "Nice to know what you think of my size, Clea, but no. That was hours ago." He winked just before Houston popped him in the back of his head.

"Don't be talking to Clea about your dick."

"She brought it up," Dallas whined before turning narrowed eyes back on me. "You saw him there." He accused.

I shrugged. "I didn't know what he was going to do." I winked back at him, and Dallas threw his hands up in the air and turned to stalk off while mumbling.

"He's going to marry that one, and I'll be stuck with Satan for a sister-in-law."

I couldn't help laughing until I noticed the contemplative look on his brother's face.

"That's all in his head," I shot off quickly, so he wouldn't think I planted that idea.

Houston reached out and wrapped one of his large hands around my hip. The warmth immediately radiated through my clothes and made me wish I could feel him touch me without that barrier.

"Come home with me when we're done here?"

"I drove Becs here. I need to give her a ride home." My best friend made a run to the bathroom a few minutes before and hadn't made it back yet, but Austin and Jordan were both still organizing behind the bar.

"I can take Becs home," Austin offered, and I didn't miss the scathing look Jordan threw his way. Too bad that he did, or he might have rescinded his offer.

"Why would you take me home?" The woman in question asked as she finally made her way back to my side.

"I asked Clea to come home with me when we're done closing down."

Becs looked torn for a minute, but then seemed resigned. "I don't live that far. It doesn't matter who drops me off. You should go with Houston. It was a big night and I'm sure you both want to celebrate."

I hugged my bestie and whispered in her ear, "I owe you."

Jordan threw her towel down, huffed, grabbed her bag from somewhere under the counter and took off. Austin watched her go but didn't make a move to follow after her or call the woman back. I wasn't sure what was going on with them, but it was clear Jordan wasn't happy about him giving Becs a ride.

"Be careful," I said to her.

"Aren't I always?" She teased, and I could tell it was all bluster and fake bravado.

"No, that's why I warned you."

She laughed then, a real sound that matched the ways her eyes crinkled in delight. "Whatever. I'm too tired to not be careful."

About an hour later, we finally managed to get finished with everything and I hopped into my car to follow Houston to his house. At first, I thought maybe he had been given my address by someone because it looked like we were headed back to my house. Then we turned and ended up two streets over from where I lived. The house we pulled up to was almost identical to mine, causing my jaw to drop as I exited the car.

"What's going on?"

"This looks like my house, minus the attempts I've made at gardening. Failed attempts, mind you, but it is uncanny how similar they are."

Houston surveyed the exterior of his home and then turned back to me. "Where exactly do you live?"

"Two streets back that way," I told him as I hitched my thumb over my shoulder, indicating the direction we'd just come from.

"No wonder," he said absently.

"No wonder what?"

"I've seen you around a few times. Once, it looked like you were trying to jog or maybe you were running slowly away from someone. There was this panicked gleam in your eyes," he teased.

I laughed. "So, you were just going to let me get taken by whoever was trying to get me?"

"I figured if they couldn't catch you at that rate, there wasn't really a worry," he deadpanned.

I burst out laughing. "You're an asshole."

"You came home with me."

"That I did," I admitted with a giant smile stretching my face.

"Let's go in before you change your mind and decide to slow-motion run all the way home."

"For the love of God, man! I have a car right there!" I pointed toward my vehicle. "Why would I run?"

"Just a thought," he reminded me before coming to my side and swinging me up into his arms bridal style. "Come on before Old Mr. Thompson across the street gets ideas."

"What kind of ideas would the old guy get?"

"That I don't know what to do with the beautiful woman hanging out on my lawn. I have a reputation to uphold."

"No, you don't!" An elderly male voice called out, startling us both. "Young lady, that boy hasn't seen any action, far as I can tell, in far too long. Now, don't go feeling sorry for him, but if he can't get the job done, you know where to find me."

"Thanks for the vote of confidence, Mr. Thompson," Houston called out as he quickly got me tucked away inside his house.

"Does your neighbor always sit outside at three in the morning waiting to hound you and your dates?"

"Well, as you just heard, there is usually an absence of dates, but yeah, he has insomnia and spends a lot of time on that porch. I think since he lost Mrs. Thompson, it's hard for him to be in the house where they used to live together."

"Aww that's sad," I commented with my lip poked out. I felt bad for older people who lost their spouse after a lifetime together.

"Yeah, it was even sadder when her actual husband, Mr. Thompson's brother, came to collect her." Houston started laughing at the stricken look on my face. "Just kidding, she passed away from cancer about a year ago."

I smacked his chest playfully. "That's nothing to joke about."

"Listen to some of the stories Mr. Thompson tells sometimes, I don't think I'm that far off the mark." He chuckled. "Apparently the older generation is a bit more risky and frisky than people tend to give them credit for."

"Maybe, we should change the subject now," I offered with my nose scrunched up. It wasn't quite disgust that made my face wrinkle that way, but all I could picture was my nanna and poppy doing things they should no longer be doing. That was the mood killer we didn't need the first time we managed to be alone together.

"Can I get you something to drink?" Houston asked politely.

I shook my head and moved to stand directly in front of him. "I think there's something else we both wanted to explore."

"Chemistry?"

That time, my head bobbed up and down in agreement. "Do you think the chemistry we've felt all night goes beyond just working well together?"

He smirked and pulled me closer so that the front of his body was leaning into mine enough that I could feel he was already on the same page with me. "I think we'll work well together no matter what we're doing, but if you want to test things out, I have no problem with that."

"Oh good!" I didn't get to continue our flirty banter because Houston leaned in and fused our mouths together with a blazing hot kiss that scorched me down to my toes and lit my insides on fire. I moaned into his mouth as we both parted for one another at the same time. Both of his hands found their way to my ass cheeks, and he pulled me even tighter into his body while he squeezed my ample backside. Everyone has their own hotspot erogenous zones, but having my ass squeezed like that and played with was one of my big triggers.

I groaned into his mouth and tried to climb the man so that my core would line up with his. He obliged by picking me up and carrying me through the main part of the ranch-style house, down a hall, and into the last door on the left. The master bedroom was just a bit more spacious than my own, but that's all that I noticed before being tossed onto the bed.

Propped on my elbows, I watched as Houston took his time getting out of each piece of clothing. His body was a work of art to my eyes. It didn't scream gym rat, but definitely spoke of a healthy lifestyle. I moved to disrobe as well, but a quick shake of Houston's head stilled my hands. Instead, I watched, and grew hungrier as he stripped down to nothing right before my eyes.

His cock was the last thing I allowed myself to look at, and when I did, there was no disappointment. The man was well endowed, kept himself neatly trimmed, but still held that manly edge with the happy trail from his belly button down to the prize that bobbed as he moved toward me.

"Hello to you too," I mumbled to his dick.

"What?" Houston chuckled.

"Your cock is waving hello, I thought I would acknowledge the effort."

"You're a fucking nut!" He teased and then took my mouth with his own before I could argue. Truth be told, he probably wasn't wrong. I had a bad habit of saying what I was thinking and not filtering things. "This has to go," Houston demanded while he removed the anti-cupid t-shirt I had worn tonight. "Did you wear this for me?"

"It's what your shirt said all those years ago."

"So, you did see me that night?" It was a question as he leaned down and nipped his teeth over my bra-covered nipple.

"I saw you for a second before Dallas knocked me over," I admitted. "I remembered the picture of the shirt that had been sent to Becs before we headed out though."

Houston reached underneath me to slip the clasps of my bra

free and then he dragged his hands back around, taking my bra with them as he went. "So fucking beautiful. I want to kill that asshole for fucking everything up back then."

"We're here now, so let's leave the past where it is. No regrets."

His eyes met mine, and for a moment, it was clear that we both wondered 'what if', but that it didn't matter because we were together now.

Houston's mouth opened and his warm tongue snaked out to lap at my left nipple. Then he moved to give the right the same treatment. Each time he took his mouth away, my nipples grew harder as the wet left behind from his licks met the cool air in the room. His attention soon left my breasts as he trailed open-mouthed kisses down my torso, stopping to lick playfully at my belly button while he unbuttoned my jeans and slipped the zipper down.

The metal teeth of the zipper releasing was the only other noise beyond our heavy panting breaths. If anticipation was a noise, it would have been that sound. Houston's teeth nipped lower on my belly as he slid my jeans down over my hips and ass. Another lick, suck, and tease of teeth on my sensitive lower bed made me moan and wish for his mouth to go just a little lower.

Instead, he used those teeth to tug at the lace top of my panties before digging his fingers into the flesh of my hips and then pulling down on the rest of the material still hindering his view of my lower body.

He inhaled deeply as he slowly slid the material down and I swear, I heard him growl. The fact that my body brought out his animalistic side made me wetter than I've ever been.

Then his warm breath was right there, hovering over my center, promising the end to my dry spell and so much more. Houston pushed closer, gave a little kiss right above where my clit was and then he slid down further to make sure that my legs weren't still tangled in my jeans or panties. Who cared about that? I didn't.

"Come back!" I cried out in desperation.

Houston chuckled against my thigh. "Patience my sweet Clea."

His. Sweet. Clea.

Yeah, I liked that.

Once the rest of my clothing was tossed aside, Houston crawled seductively back up my body. He placed kisses as he went and all the while, his hands stayed busy too.

"So wet!" His voice sounded deeper than it had moments ago as he trailed a finger up the seam of my pussy lips, spreading them slightly, only to pull away again and leave another kiss somewhere along my body.

"What do you want me to do with this beautiful pussy you have dripping for me, Clea?"

"Make it yours?" I suggested, though it sounded more like a question. He laughed and then took a swipe at my needy center with his tongue.

"Why does that feel like heaven?" I asked.

"Tastes like heaven, sweet Clea."

I ran my fingers down the side of my body until they made contact with his. Our hands joined on one side for a moment as my other drifted into his hair. "Then you won't mind staying right there for just a bit, yeah?"

He chuckled again, this time without lifting his face away from my vagina and damn if the vibrations didn't send me into another level of bliss. Both hands were in his hair without me realizing I'd put them there in a solid attempt to guide the man to where I really needed him.

He licked again and when I moaned, he seemed to lose whatever patience had allowed him to tease me up to that point. Instead of quick swipes of his tongue, Houston dove in and went to town eating my pussy like a starving man who had just been seated at an all you can eat buffet.

"Holy shit!" I yelped when he sucked my clit into his mouth and then nibbled on it lightly with his teeth before letting go and driving his tongue inside me. It didn't take long before he was attacking my clit with that divine mouth of his again while he primed me with a couple fingers. The come-hither motion he rocked against that spongy little area inside me caused my hips to jack up and push his face further into my pussy. Then, he pushed down slightly on my lower abdomen and I shot off like a fireworks display at an Independence Day celebration. I don't think I'd ever seen twinkling lights when I came before, but I knew for a fact that I'd never squirted before and here we were, with Houston between my legs reveling in the fact that I was soaking the hell out of his comforter.

"Fucking hell, you are perfect for me!" His declaration almost fell on deaf ears as another wave of pleasure rolled through me when Houston pushed up on that special spot once more before pulling out and plopping them right into his mouth to lick up my mess.

"Oh Clea, I hope you know that I'm never letting you go after this."

"That's good, because, same," I panted the words out in an unsteady rhythm.

Houston managed to splay his body out on top of mine before dipping his mouth toward mine and letting me taste the fruits of his labor. I was both sweet and tangy on his tongue, and hotter for him than I had ever been for any man in my life.

"Fuck me," I whispered against his lips, and he moved to comply before jerking back.

"Shit!" He hissed as he stared down at me with wide eyes.

"What?"

"I almost forgot a condom."

"Oh!" It was my turn to be shocked, because so had I. After what I'd just endured with my ex, including the humiliation of having to go be screened for sexually transmitted diseases, I couldn't believe that almost happened.

"Stay there," Houston demanded. "I'll be right back," he called back after leaping off the bed and running from the room. I laughed at his eager flight, but wondered where in the hell he kept the condoms considering we were in his bedroom and there was a master bath attached.

"Fuck!" I heard him yell from somewhere else in the house before he showed up again with an empty box of condoms. My eyebrows flew into my hairline as I thought about what that must mean.

"Fucking Dallas!" He growled again and then my brows relaxed as I laughed at our predicament.

"Little brother strikes again. I swear it's like he hated me before he knew me," I complained.

"I should have never let him stay here after his apartment was flooded."

"I don't even want to know how that happened." I glanced down at Houston's flagging cock and jutted my lip out in a very real pout. "We could go to my place. I think I might have some there."

"Seriously?"

I stood up and started getting dressed. "It's only just down the road. It's either that or check in with Mr. Thompson next door and see if he has any," I laughed as I said it, but Houston looked contemplative.

"Come on, it won't take long, and then I can rock your world the way you just did mine."

"Clea, I have news for you… The way you soaked my bed did rock my world."

I blushed from the roots of my hair down to my toes as he reminded me about my squirting incident. "I've never done that before," I admitted.

"That just makes it even better. Let's get out of here before I take my chances without protection."

"I'm clean," I insisted as we left his house.

"Me too, and I figured you'd been tested after what happened, but..." He left things hanging there and I knew what 'but' meant.

"We don't know one another well enough to risk Houston Junior?" I questioned teasingly.

"That will never be our son's name," was his retort, as if it was a foregone conclusion that we would, in fact, one day have a son.

8

It was a shame that when we got back to my place on Valentine's Day – or I suppose technically it was the morning after – that there were no condoms to be found there either. Apparently, I had thrown them all out with Jeff's shit when I packed his things up for him. I didn't leave Houston hanging though. He got one amazing blow job, and I got the promise of our first real date a week later. Yes, a week. Our schedules sucked.

What didn't suck was our first date.

"Where exactly are you taking me?"

"It's a surprise," Houston answered. While I couldn't see him through the phone, only hear his voice, it was clear that he was amused with my pestering demands that he tell me where we were going on our first date.

"How am I supposed to dress?"

"Well, I have several options, based on weather and how you dress. So, you dress for how you're feeling, and I promise, it will be appropriate for wherever we end up."

"What if I dress in my birthday suit?"

"Then I guess we'll be staying in for our first date."

"You're too easy," I teased.

"Only for you, Clea. Don't forget that."

It was a good thing he couldn't see me get all swoony.

"Pick you up at six, sweet girl."

"See you then, handsome."

I could have sworn I heard a growl on the other end of the line before he hung up. That growly sound he made was a panty-dropper for sure. I decided that I shouldn't tell him about that though because then he would have way more power over me than I had over him.

Then again, letting Houston Mercer be in charge didn't exactly sound like a bad idea to me.

I decided to go with a dressier casual look, because despite what Houston said, and unless he was bringing a change of clothes, he had to be dressing for something specific. I put on black denim pants and an ivory blouse that dipped low into my cleavage, draped loosely on my shoulders, and had stays that held the billowy sleeves rolled up to about three-quarter length. I paired them with some black pumps and a gold Pave Fossil necklace that was wrapped in diamonds. It was something my mother had given me when I graduated from university. Had I known how much she paid for it, I never would have accepted. Since I rarely wore it, knowing what it was worth, a first date with the man I had high hopes for seemed like the lucky time to break it out.

I had to laugh when I opened the door later to find Houston standing there in dark jeans, a white button-down shirt with gold and black vertical lines blown through it. We couldn't have matched better if we had tried. He took me in from top to toe and chuckled as well.

"Well, it looks like my skills as a psychic are now indisputable," I joked.

"You are stunning, Clea." Houston handed me a red, pink, and white lily and rose bouquet of flowers in a crystal vase.

"They're absolutely gorgeous!" I cooed as I took the flowers and placed them in the middle of my coffee table, so they'd be the first thing I saw when I returned to my house.

"I'm glad you like them."

"Lilies are my favorite."

His smile grew when he heard that. "I'll remember from now on."

The whole way to the restaurant, Houston held my leg or my hand. It was sweet and showed that he was with me, even when he concentrated on his driving. The radio played some old blues while the purely masculine scent of him all over the car continued to remind me of our one intimate night together. His signature citrusy scent had the slightest hint of pepper to it too and while I never thought about such a combination being a turn on, the spicy, citrus notes mixed with Houston's own natural scent drove me absolutely wild.

"What kind of cologne do you wear?" I finally asked just as we were pulling into the parking lot outside of a Mediterranean restaurant called The Olive Branch. I had never been there before, but it was on my list of places to try, especially since they also catered small to midsize events.

"Sauvage. My sister got it for me a couple years ago, and I've been using it ever since." Worry creased his brow after his explanation before he asked, "Why, do you like it?"

"Oh, don't worry, handsome. I love it."

"Sit tight," he said as a smirk immediately replaced his worry and did funny things to my lady parts and kept me squirming in my seat as Houston got out, rounded the car, and came to open my door for me.

Once we were inside, and seated across the small table from one another, Houston grabbed my hand and held it there. "I hope this is okay?"

"I've never been here before, so you might have to help me figure out what's good, but I love the ambiance," I told him as I glanced around.

"I can do that. You don't have any allergies or things you absolutely won't eat, do you?"

"Nope. I'm an adventurous eater and have no allergies, thank God!" I knocked on wood with my free hand because the way my luck had been running for the past few years, I didn't like to tempt fate.

"Perfect." When my eyes returned to our table to meet his, he smiled even wider. "Absolutely fucking perfect," he added, and there was no doubt he was talking about me as a whole and not just my appetite and lack of food issues.

"So, why did you choose this place?"

"As you said, it has great ambiance. It's really laid back, but classy still." That made me wonder how many other women he had brought here, but as if he could read that on my face, he shook his head. "My mother brought me here a few weeks ago when my dad was too busy to keep their reservations. I didn't even realize this place existed before then."

"Well, thank your mother for me then because it's been on my list of places to try for a while since they cater for events."

"How did you get into event planning and what else is it that you do? Modeling or you're an agent?"

I smiled at his confusion because he wasn't alone. My business was an oddly eclectic one.

"The event planning actually helped launch the rest of what I do. I know it seems weird to people, but as you saw with the club opening, sometimes everything just fits perfectly into place and if my business wasn't shaped the way it is, I would have to hire a lot of aspects of my job out to other people. So, we have the modeling division, where we represent local talent, then we have our in-house photographers, videographers, and state of the art marketing team who are pros at putting together business launches, ad campaigns, book launches, and whatever else our clients might need."

"I think it's rather impressive that you're able to be that multi-faceted."

"I've worked hard at my business and didn't want to turn anyone down because we couldn't accommodate their needs."

Houston seemed impressed and over the course of dinner and dessert, we played the get-to-know you game by taking turns asking the other what we wanted to know. It was a wonderful date with the undercurrent of sexual tension in every touch, smile, and thoughtful compliment. Okay, fine. We were both horny little shits who were trying desperately to have a polite date before getting to the good stuff.

"Are you ready to get out of here?" Houston asked as he stood from the table and held his hand out for me to take.

"I'm so past ready," I admitted, which made him chuckle.

We left the restaurant and headed back to Houston's home. I flushed, half embarrassed, half anticipation when I thought about what happened the last time we were there.

"You can bet your ass that we're going to get a repeat performance," he promised as he got out of his car and came around to fetch me from my side. Chivalry was so not dead with this man. In the six years that I was with Jeff, he never once opened a car door for me, let alone any other door unless it was by accident. I should have known how selfish he was then. Don't get me wrong, I can get my feminist boots on just like any other person out there, but common courtesy should still apply in relationships. I don't mind holding the door either, but it's nice to know someone is there looking out for you.

"Better treat that girl right!" A man's disembodied voice called out to us. I glanced over to see Mr. Thompson sitting in the shadows of his porch.

"How are you today, Mr. Thompson?" I called back to him.

"Be better if you leave that schmuck and come keep me company instead."

"No can do, Mr. Thompson. Houston was just about to show me how to play on a waterbed."

"Boy! You have a waterbed over there? I thought those things died out in the eighties."

"No, sir, I do not," Houston responded with the biggest grin ever on his face.

"Oh shit!" I heard Mr. Thompson mumble as Houston quickly ushered me inside his home and slammed the door shut behind us.

"Oh, you naughty girl, you are going to have to live up to that challenge now. Better go grab us a couple bottles of water to put beside the bed while I get the condoms," he teased. Or maybe he wasn't teasing, since he pointed toward the kitchen where the water bottles were stashed.

I grabbed four bottles of water. It might have been overkill, but after the way Houston made me gush the last time we were together, I figured it was better safe than sorry. When I got to the bedroom it was to find the man turning on a bunch of battery-operated candles.

"Safety first in all ways, huh?" I joked.

He laughed as he set the last one down. "I don't plan on just sticking to the bed, so I figured it was better not to burn the place down around us."

Oddly enough, there wasn't anything awkward about our sex-fest prepping. It just seemed as though it was something we had always done. There was a familiarity to the process that shouldn't have been there.

"We fit," he said, as if he read my mind once again. "Come here." I moved to him without any hesitation. Again, because it did feel like we fit. He was a comfortable place to land and explore and just be with.

"I want you naked," I demanded once firmly ensconced in his arms.

"You first this time." He flipped my blouse up over my head and tossed it onto a chair that sat beside the window and a bookshelf that I hadn't noticed last time, but wanted to explore. Once Houston and I had enough of one another, it was imperative to see what kind of books he chose to keep around. You could tell a lot about a person by the things they read.

"You are so fucking beautiful, Clea." Houston's praise made me feel so special. It didn't matter that he was in the process of stripping me naked. The reverent tone in his voice told me it was more than just the impending sex. That was truly how he saw me.

My bra, pumps, jeans, and panties all came off, followed closely by Houston's shoes and shirt. He left his pants on as he sat me on the edge of his bed and then pushed the middle of my chest with enough effort to tip me over on my back. He took my legs and positioned them so I was splayed out before him with my feet holding me up at the edge of the bed and my bottom very close to dangling over.

"Ah, perfect!" he murmured as the man got down on his knees before me and leaned in toward my sex. "A feast fit for a king."

"Oh God!" I cried out because he didn't waste a moment and instead dove in and got busy doing exactly that. He feasted on me. Between his mouth and those magic fucking hands of his, I was coming in no time. The first time, without the waterworks. The second time though, he pressed down on my lower abdomen at the same time he stroked upward on that spongy spot inside me, and I was gushing. Truthfully, the gushing part didn't even register so much for me because my ears were ringing and I saw stars once again as the immense pleasure barreled through me in unexpected waves of pure bliss. The man still hadn't put his cock inside of me and he was already the best sex I ever had.

"I need you, Houston."

"Almost there, sweet Clea." I picked my head up long enough

to see that he was sheathing himself in a condom before he leaned forward and slammed himself home into my center. The sheer fullness of him being inside me for the first time took my breath away.

"You okay?" He asked, his words came out a little choppy as he kept himself sheathed to the hilt inside me.

"Perfect," I whimpered as he pulled out just a bit and slammed back in.

"Feel that?" He asked.

I nodded my head and reached up to pinch my own nipples since his hands were wrapped firmly around my hips to keep me from falling off the end of the bed or scooting too far away.

"You feel me so fucking deep inside you, baby?"

I had no words, just more nods and as he started hammering in and out of me at a relentless pace. His balls slapped against my ass on each inward thrust and he swiveled his hips while leaning forward so that his pubic bone stimulated my clit too.

"God! Houston! What? I can't... Oh shit!" I yelled out nonsense. Absolute fucking nonsense. The man was literally fucking me stupid and I didn't mind one damn bit. Suddenly, I wondered if this was how bimbos were made. You know the girls portrayed in books and movies who were too stupid to live, but always down to fuck? Yeah, them. I understood and would never judge them again.

"Clea," Houston called my name and when our eyes connected, he moved just so that he was once again thrusting forward, slowly that time, and rubbing against every sensitive spot I had. "Pull those nipples for me," he demanded as he continued his assault on my senses. "That's it, my sweet girl. You feel that?" As I tugged, he pushed forward and hit my clit with his pubic bone again. The zing of pleasure that moved through my body was insane.

"Yeah," I groaned. "Don't stop. Whatever you're doing... just... don't... stop! Oh God!" I had never been very vocal during sex, and I was beginning to think it was because I had never been dicked down this fucking good before.

"Houston!"

"Clea!" My name was a breathy response from him as he panted. Then he snatched my legs off the bed, threw them over his shoulders and basically bent me in half as our torsos nearly met and he started thrusting even harder than before.

Dear God, is that my cervix? There was a pinch of pain each time he drilled down into me, but it was coupled with a pleasurable, almost electrical charge too that made my eyes roll back in my head for just a moment.

"Fuuuuck! Clea, I need," Houston started to say, but then he dragged one hand down between us and used it to torment my clit as he dipped his head, sucked and nibbled my neck and shoulder. That was it. I didn't know how in the hell the man was performing the circus act that he managed, but every single one of my erogenous zones came to life, zipped with energy, and then released all at once. And I was fucking done.

"Clea?" I heard my name being called, but refused to open my eyes. "Clea?" He called again. Languidly, I allowed my lids to part just enough so that I could see Houston's concerned face staring down into my own. "You good?"

"Better than," I managed to say.

My own personal sex God then picked me up and slid me into a more comfortable position with my head resting on the pillows at the top of the bed, then he climbed in beside me and tossed a light blanket over us as our bodies began to cool under the breeze coming from the ceiling fan. I glanced up curiously wondering if it had been on the whole time or not.

"I thought you overheated, so I flipped it on. You passed out for a minute there."

"Blissed out brain overload. I'm fine, but I probably can't move on my own for a while since my bones turned to liquid."

"You're killing me Clea." Houston leaned over and kissed my

lips in what was probably meant to be a simple chaste kiss until I deepened it.

"It's a good way to die," I mumbled there against his mouth.

He pulled back as he chuckled. "Good to know that chemistry works in all aspects of our life, huh?"

"Doesn't matter. I vote we never leave the house again."

"If only we were both independently wealthy."

"Damn. Life is a bitch!"

Surprisingly enough, we managed a round two once my bones reformed and drank some water. Round two was extra special because my beautiful sex God took me from behind and played with my ass. He had me coming so quickly it should have been embarrassing, but then again, he followed right behind me. That's where things got a little messy, considering how new our relationship was.

"Um, Clea?" He questioned. I turned my head just enough to see him looking down toward where he had just pulled out of me. Panic set in. At first, I wondered if maybe I hadn't cleaned well enough. Maybe there was tissue still stuck to my butt or something? We had that one-ply bullshit at work because my stupid ex-assistant ordered cases of the awful stuff before she was fired for fucking my ex-fiancé in my office.

Maybe I started my period early and was bleeding?

About twenty more awful, what the fuck, scenarios floated through my mind before I glanced back up and my eyes met with Houston's.

"What?" I asked, despite the dread I felt in my belly.

"He held up the condom he'd just taken off, but something seemed wrong. First of all, there was the drip. Then, it registered that the entire tip of the condom appeared to be missing.

"What in the hell is that?"

"The condom broke."

"I can see that. How in the hell does the whole end just fall off like that?" I shrieked as I turned over and sat up. That movement did nothing but highlight the problem as Houston's warm cum was overtaken by gravity and started to flow right back out of my pussy.

"Oh God!"

"Are you on the pill?"

"No," I groaned. "When everything happened with Jeff, I stopped taking it, because you're supposed to take breaks off the hormones sometimes, you know?"

He shook his head, obviously not knowing that little tidbit.

"Well, it's a thing. I didn't think I'd end up with anyone. I swore off men. You were the exception I didn't expect."

Houston suddenly swooped in and kissed the absolute hell out of me. "I was the exception, huh?" He asked when he finally let me come up for air.

"Yeah." The word came out as soft as a cloud as all the worry about what might happen slipped away in the wake of that kiss and the look on Houston's face at that moment.

"We'll just have to wait and see, but Clea, I'm here. No matter what. I'm not going anywhere."

ॐ

IT WAS JUST over two weeks later, and we were still on period watch, as I should have been starting sometime soon, when Houston and I decided to try the new Thai food place that opened in the mall food court. The first mistake we made was Thai food when I was already dealing with a nervous stomach. The second mistake we made was Thai food from the mall's food court.

Considering the fact that we were on period watch, wondering if a broken condom at the wrong time of the month might have gotten me pregnant, it did not bode well when I had to run to the bathroom the minute we got in the door of Houston's house.

I was head down, hovering over the toilet bowl when my stomach rumbled so hard it actually ached. I hoped like hell this was not what morning sickness felt like. It was awful. I started throwing up again, and Houston was there, holding my hair back and putting a cold washcloth on the back of my neck. When I heaved the next time, something happened. An evil seal inside me was broken and hell bent on my complete humiliation because while I was mid vomit, my butt decided it would be a good time to join the nasty party as well.

If I could have screamed out a warning, I would have. Instead, I was midway through choking on vomit as I started to shit myself. All while Houston was holding my hair back. This was something that was not supposed to happen to a couple until they had been married for like 50 years and it was a foregone conclusion that the need for adult diapers was imminent.

Once all the vomit was out, I moaned a loud lament and got ready to apologize when Houston ran from the room, clearly disgusted with what he had just been forced to witness. I was wearing pants, so it wasn't like I blasted my ass and shit all over his leg or anything. But the smell. Oh God! The smell.

And before I could move to clean myself up, I was back to heaving into the toilet. Oh, happy fucking days. The only good thing about my predicament was that I didn't think these exact symptoms were anything to do with a surprise pregnancy, especially when I stopped puking only to hear Houston take up the mantle.

By the time I got myself picked up, peeled out of my shitty pants, and into the shower, Houston had finally made his way back into the master bath. "I tried calling Austin to bring us some clear fluids and soup, but I couldn't get through."

"That's probably for the best. We'll just die together so we never, ever have to speak of this happening again. I glanced out of the shower curtain in time to see Houston's face turn green as he looked at my shitastrophy that used to be my Lucky Brand jeans. They were the ones that made my booty pop the best too. Maybe, it was okay to cry in the shower in front of your boyfriend after shitting your pants? Yeah, it probably was.

When Houston was done puking, he peeked into the shower. "How do we get them clean enough to throw in the wash?" He asked. Then, in answer to his own question, "I guess we could try to get them outside and hose them down?" The dubious look on his face told me he wasn't exactly volunteering for that job.

It was at that point that I lost it. I doubled over and laughed so hard that I farted, right there in the shower and even sick. Houston's reflexes were something to be envied because he slammed the shower curtain shut, blocking the blast radius of my asshole, so that he wouldn't get hit by anything that might come flying out.

I was mortified!

Thankfully, it was only a fart!

"It's all clear," I called out amidst a burst of laughter.

"As in, there's nothing coming out, or you're shitting clear?" He asked while also trying to contain his own laughter.

"Oh God! I'm never coming out of this shower again. Just throw some food in periodically. We'll pretend I'm a glorified pet or something," I mumbled. "Like a fucking turtle you keep in your bathtub because it keeps shitting itself."

Houston's laughter grew louder just as someone else's voice caught my attention. "I was just around the corner, and fuck am I thankful it was me you called!"

"No! Tell me you didn't call Cupid to the rescue!" I groaned.

"I told you Austin was busy."

"No!"

"Are those pants full of shit?" Dallas asked his brother.

"Bad mall Thai food," Houston said by way of explanation.

"What kind of cheap date are you, that you took your girl to the mall for poisoned Thai food?"

Houston's response was to start hurling again. I could have sworn I heard Dallas gagging too.

"I'll just ask Mom what I should get for you guys. Be back," he called out and was already far enough away that he had to yell to be heard over Houston's heaves.

"He's telling your mother," I cried. "The woman who I have not met yet will have this as her first impression of me. I'm that girl! The one who shits her pants at 27."

9

As it turned out, Dallas ended up getting some of the best homemade chicken soup from his mother to bring back to us, along with an invitation to come meet her, and the rest of the family, in person for Sunday dinner as soon as we were both feeling better. My initial reaction was that I would never be feeling better, thanks to my complete mortification over the shit-splosion that happened in my pants while my head was firmly planted inside a toilet bowl. Why? Dear God, why did that have to happen with Houston standing right there?

"Stop thinking about it," Houston demanded before taking another careful sip of his Gatorade. My poor, filthy Lucky Brand jeans had been bagged up and taken out to the garbage to help eliminate the sick smell in the house, and also because – gross!

"You didn't shit yourself in front of me," I whined.

"No, because I learned from your mistake, parked my ass on the toilet and held the waste bin in front of my face."

"You suck!" I stuck my tongue out at him. "And you're welcome for that tip, by the way."

We both chuckled lightly, afraid to fully laugh at the situation, lest it end up a shitty mess again.

Houston's phone pinged with an incoming message that broke up our near-miss laugh fest about the food poisoning debacle.

"Shit," he grumped.

"What?"

"Turns out that Austin wasn't really working the bar last night when he sent Dallas."

"What's that mean?"

"Austin left Jordan in charge and took off to meet up with your friend."

"Becs?" I gasped, because Becs hadn't said anything yet.

"Yeah, they went to Austin's house and hooked up, but Jordan stopped by after work and now she's throwing a fucking fit. Austin said that Becs snuck out in the middle of them arguing and he asked that you check on her."

"Why can't he check on her, since he made the mess?"

"I think Jordan might have put her foot down."

"Are they dating?"

Houston shook his head. "Not that I know of, but they have this weird thing. I guess it's a fuck buddy situation with a stipulation that if they don't both find someone by the time they're thirty, they'll get married."

"Lovely, so basically whenever your brother tries to find someone else, she interferes to keep him free and clear until he's obligated?"

Houston blinked at me and then grimaced down at his phone. "I hadn't thought about it that way, but you might be onto something there."

I scoffed at him. "It didn't take a genius to figure out, Houston." My phone sat idle with no messages, so I decided to take the proactive friend approach without letting on that I knew anything.

Clea: How was your night? I got food poisoning, tell you about it when I see you.

Nothing came back for a few minutes. Then, finally, Becs texted.

Becs: Will you be home after lunch? I stopped by, but I'm guessing you're at lover man's place.

Clea: I can leave now if you need me.

Becs: No, I'll see you for lunch.

Clea: Okay, see you then, but I'll probably just be on a liquid diet, so no need to bring food for both of us.

Becs: No need for food then. Gotcha.

My heart ached for my best friend. That didn't sound good. The only time she lost her appetite was when her heart was broken or she was really nervous about something.

"I'm going to have to head out soon so I can meet up at my house with Becs."

"I figured," Houston said as he leaned over and kissed me on the forehead. "Sorry our night ended the way it did," he added.

I laughed. "You and me both."

"Do you want a pair of sweats to wear home since…" It was nice of him to leave the demise of my jeans hanging and not bring it up again.

"I would be grateful and promise not to muck them up."

Houston sputtered and then that turned into a full-blown laugh as he gingerly got out of bed and moved toward his dresser to grab me a pair of sweats. Once I was dressed and ready to go,

Houston stopped me with his hand wrapped around my bicep and a serious look on his face.

"Promise me something?"

"What's that?"

"Whatever is going on with Becs and Austin, can we make sure it stays with them and doesn't become our problem too?"

"They're both grownups, Houston. I love my best friend. I never want to see her hurt, but if she is, you aren't the one that did that to her and she wouldn't want me to treat you badly because of it. She already knows how that feels, since that's the excuse your brother gave for ghosting her the last time."

Houston nodded. "That's what I was worried about. It's been done to her. I didn't want…"

"It won't get turned around on you, I promise. I'll be there for her, just like I'm sure you'll be there for Austin, but what's between them is exactly that."

"Not so sure I want to be there for my brother, considering this mess is all his making."

"He's still your brother, whether he's an idiot or not."

Houston grinned at me then. "Now, I truly know I have nothing to worry about."

"You never did."

❧

Two hours later, I wanted to tie Houston's brother to the railroad tracks, old-school cartoon style and let the trains have at him. I didn't understand how Austin could be the older brother. Honestly, my opinion of him after speaking to Becs actually put him lower than Dallas, and I never thought that would happen.

"Did he at least text you or call to make sure you got home safely?"

"No, and he's the one that drove me to his house. I walked three blocks from his place before I could even call for an Uber to come get me. Then I had to wait there for the guy to show up, and to top off my miserable morning he was playing show tunes on the stereo."

"What do you have against show tunes? You like musicals."

"Sure, when the people singing them can actually sing, but you didn't let me get to the part where my driver thought it was a ride and a show. He was singing along at the top of his lungs, and it wasn't pretty. It wasn't even ugly, Clea. It was so awful that I think a little bit of my brain might have leaked out of my ears in an attempt to escape."

It physically hurt me to try to hold my laughter in, but I managed. Instead, I decided to humiliate myself further in an effort to make my friend feel better about her day.

"That's nothing compared to my night of torture."

"What? I thought you were with Houston?"

"I was. We stupidly ate Thai food at the mall," I started and could tell by her wince that she agreed with Dallas that it had been the first place we had gone wrong. Then I told her about my shitty night.

"Oh my God! Clea!" Becs had tears rolling down her face and was holding onto her stomach because she laughed so hard that it hurt. Apparently, I shouldn't have held back when she was talking about her show tune singing Uber driver making her bleed brains from her ears.

"You're an asshole! Why are you laughing? I was throwing up and shitting myself in front of my boyfriend and my favorite pair of jeans are now history."

"Clea, I'm so sorry," she hiccuped through her apology because she laughed so hard that she apparently upset her diaphragm too. "At least Houston was understanding and also sick, so he really knew what you were going through."

"Yeah, there is that." I chuckled and then turned to pull her into a hug. "I'm sorry that you don't have that too. I know you had hoped…"

"Hope is a bitch that I wish I could meet one day, just so I could punch her in the face."

"Remind me to screen new people for you from now on, just in case."

She rolled her eyes at me. "You know what I mean." The sigh that left her then felt a lot like defeat.

"Maybe it's time to give up on him completely. I know you've dated, but there hasn't been anyone serious since Austin."

"I don't know, Clea. Maybe, I'm meant to be alone."

"No one is meant to be alone for life, Becs. Just because one guy was a complete tool and didn't know how to drop his childhood bestie, fuck buddy, or whatever the hell she is to him, that doesn't mean the rest of them are like that."

TWO DAYS LATER, I had my work cut out for me in the best friend department, because Becs hadn't left her apartment since she got back from lunch with me days ago.

I knocked on her door. "Becs, open up, or I'm using my key and I'll feel really bad if you're in there boning some hot dude instead of just feeling sorry for yourself!"

Her neighbor, who happened to be a hot dude, laughed as he made his way past me from his own apartment. Damn my timing.

"Your friend is hot. Tell her if she needs help getting over someone, she can get under me."

"I don't know whether that's chivalrous or gross," I admitted.

He waved his hands down the length of his own body and tipped his head to the side as if to say, 'definitely not gross'. He was missing the point.

"I'll pass that on to her," I told him and watched as he walked off. Then I banged on Becs' door again. "Your neighbor just offered to get under you. You need to open up before everyone in the building starts making an attempt at helping you get over someone."

The door creaked open and Becs looked awful.

"Okay, first thing, you're getting a shower. Then, we're going to a movie to get lost in someone else's drama for a while."

"How is that going to make me feel better?"

"One – you'll be clean. Two – you need to get out of the house. Three – we are not letting the asshole win!"

"Fine!" She agreed and hauled her butt to the bathroom to hopefully get clean. "No rom-coms though. Fuck love!"

"Yeah! Fuck love!" I yelled back.

"Shut up, you liar!" She hollered back and I was just happy to hear her trying to make a joke in the midst of her heart hurting.

An hour later, we finally made it to the theater, and ended up getting tickets to see the latest action flick because yummy heart-throbs don't fall under the 'fuck love' movement. We can still drool over them, according to Becs. We got our tub of buttered popcorn, two large drinks, and headed to the theater. The lights were still up when we went in, which I was grateful for in theory because it made it easier to find the seats that weren't a sticky mess from previous audiences.

Unfortunately, it also allowed us to see everyone else in the theater, including Austin, who was sucking face with Jordan three rows up from where we were about to sit down. I glared at the asshole who I once-upon-a-time ago found charming. My poor best friend, who needed to be convinced to leave home, had to come to the movie to see these two assholes making out like they were still in high school and came to the theater because they couldn't get in boob squeezes with their parents around.

"What a fucking douche!" I said a little too loudly, causing the tongue-tangled duo to glance over and see a pale-faced, heart-broken Becs and her angry best friend standing there staring at them. Jordan smirked. Austin looked gutted. But fuck his response. He was the one at the theater sucking face with another woman – after sexing up my bestie days ago and then ghosting her again after Jordan showed up.

"Becs!" Austin called, but my bestie had already gathered herself, and was moving back out of the theater. She dumped her popcorn and drink into the trashcan on the way out and I followed suit in solidarity.

"Becs!" Austin yelled, his voice sounding closer. I spun on my heel and stopped him from getting any closer to my friend as she left the theater.

"Go on home Becs, I'll get a ride there in a minute."

She nodded and kept going while I blocked Austin's path. "You are the biggest asshole I have ever met."

"You don't know him!" Jordan huffed at me.

"You – shut the fuck up. I'm not speaking to you right now." My angry eyes tracked from Jordan's shocked face to Austin's increasingly angry one. "My best friend didn't deserve what you did to her all those years ago, and don't you dare try to claim that it was in solidarity with your brother. I'd bet good fucking money that a certain woman was in your ear, giving you that bad fucking advice because she didn't want to lose you, and that was exactly what was happening." The way Austin glared over his shoulder at Jordan told me I was one hundred percent right in my assumptions.

"My friend didn't deserve you playing more games with her again the other night either."

"I wasn't playing games with anyone."

"Really, Austin? So, you slept with her, then your childhood fuck buddy shows up and you miss the fact that Becs even left your house, and when you did realize, you couldn't be bothered to check on her, to let her know what happened, or at least let her down easily? Instead, you ghosted her again, and after I finally convinced her to shower and leave the house to help heal her heart, what happens? We walk in on you right as fucking rain, sucking face with the woman who is always at the center of you brushing my bestie off like she's the dirt under your shoes! Grow the fuck up, Austin, and leave Becs alone. She deserves a real man who can make her happy, not a little boy who doesn't know how to fucking decide between his past and his future."

I spun around and left the two of them standing there in the theater. Becs hadn't gone far. In fact, she had been close enough to hear everything I'd just yelled at her ex-boyfriend. "Thanks for that," she whispered.

I put my arm around her, and even knowing that Austin had stepped out into the hallway and was watching us walk away, I made sure to shield her from his view. Maybe I was doomed to hate two of my future brothers-in-law. Yeah, that was an odd thought, since Houston and I hadn't been dating that long, but it felt right to think that we could be headed in that direction.

On the way home, my phone rang, and I answered through the Bluetooth. "Hello?"

"Hey sweet Clea." Houston's voice sent shivers down my spine in the best way possible.

"Hello, handsome. What can I do for you?"

"My brother just called me," he said.

I decided to play stupid. "Oh yeah? Which one?"

Becs snorted, which was her attempt at not laughing. It didn't really work. I was thankful for that too. Anything that could put a smile on her face was okay in my book.

"I think you know the one. The biggest asshole of the bunch."

"Well, a week ago, I would have said Dallas deserved that title, but this week, I'm going to assume you're talking about Austin."

"That would be the one."

"Are you calling to fuss at me for yelling at him and Jordan?"

"Nope. Just wanted to check and make sure you and Becs were okay."

"Seriously?" Becs asked. Her jaw was hanging wide open in obvious shock.

"I'm sorry that my brother hasn't managed to get his head out of his ass and act like the man he's supposed to be. So, yeah, I'm serious when I say that checking on you was a priority."

"I'll be okay," Becs murmured before she went back to staring blankly out the window.

"I know you will be," he told her, but I don't think that got through. "Will you be staying with Becs the rest of the night, Clea?"

"I think that's for the best, handsome."

"If you need anything, I will be happy to play delivery driver and then leave you both to it. From what I hear, you didn't even get to eat your popcorn at the movies. How about I bring some by, with some ice cream, and..."

"How are you so perfect?" I asked before he could finish.

"I'm not. I just want to help." There was a sound similar to his chuckling in the background for a minute. "You forget, I also have sisters. I know what they needed when they felt the same way."

"We'll be at my place, just in case someone tries to find Becs at hers," I told him. "And thank you for being amazing." We hung up after that and Becs settled in for the quiet ride home.

I hated that she got to see the sweetest possible side of Austin's brother when the scene at the movie theater was fresh in her mind. If I were her, I'd be wondering why one was not like the other. At least, I hoped that remained the case, for my boyfriend's part. If he ever pulled the things Austin had, there would be no way I would ever forgive him. No way. He would be relegated to my past and my nightmares, the same way Jeff had been.

10

"I thought you got your period already, and you guys were in the clear about the broken condom thing?"

"Becs! I only spotted for like two days. That's not normal for me. What if I was wrong and I really am pregnant?"

"Okay, but you haven't had any symptoms, other than one light period."

"So?"

"So?" Becs mocked. "Why all the tests?"

"I'm nervous. What if I'm one of those women who just never knows they're pregnant and then the next thing you know I'm walking down the snack food aisle in the grocery store – to satisfy my cravings – and bam, it looks like I'm pissing myself, except my water just broke?"

"You have such a good imagination that maybe you should think about writing books instead of doing marketing for authors."

"You're an asshole. It could happen."

"Prom babies happen because those girls are in denial. You might be sort of stacked in the boob and butt department, but I think you'd notice if your tiny little waist started expanding enough to fit a whole baby."

"I just want to be sure," I whined to my best friend.

"Fine," she hummed and grabbed a test out of the pile. "Since we're stupidly taking pregnancy tests for no good reason, I'll take one with you. Solidarity my bestie!"

I giggled as we both went our separate ways to take the test in different bathrooms. We reconverged with the tests and put them down on the counter after I dropped several layers of paper towels there. Seriously, we just peed on those sticks. I don't care if they get capped afterward. I shivered thinking about the pee that was possibly creeping toward my kitchen counter. Instead, we started talking about the past month.

It had been amazing for me. Houston and I spent the night at either my place or his at least half of the week, depending on our schedules. Becs hadn't gotten back on the dating horse yet, but she was doing much better. We had a standing date to go to the gym every morning to keep her depression away and make sure we were both staying in shape. I wasn't sure why we hadn't been doing that regularly before, but it was one of the few good things that came from the whole Austin debacle.

Having Becs take the test with me was kind of embarrassing, since it proved her point. She had been on a dry run for months before she and Austin had that one night together, and now, a month later, she was once again back to the dry spell. Obviously, she wasn't pregnant. Neither was I. It was like I knew before even glancing at the test sitting on the counter. Oddly enough, there was an empty feeling inside me when I thought about it.

Maybe, that was why I had gone a little nutso and went out to buy some tests. Part of me needed to know for sure that the possibility was no longer there so I could deal with it and move on.

I heard a click, but ignored it as my cell phone dinged, letting us know time was up and we could check the results. We both lifted our tests and my heart sank when mine was clearly negative. I plopped it back on the paper towel bed and turned to Becs. All the color had drained from her face as she stood there staring at the test. I grabbed it out of her hands and looked down to see that, unlike my own test, hers had come back positive.

"No," she whimpered.

I smelled the familiar notes of citrus and spice just before I heard, "Marry me!"

I spun to see Houston standing there with his eyes trained on the test that was now being held in my fingers between our two bodies.

"Okay," I answered without thinking why he had asked me that question. Okay? Did I really just tell the man that I would marry him? I hadn't even answered Jeff that quickly when he asked, and truth be told, I was never so sure of my answer with my ex either. Weird.

Once more, I took note of where Houston's eyes were pinned to the test I still held. "Oh, shit. No, Houston."

"No, you won't marry me?"

"No. I mean, yeah. I mean, this isn't mine!" I finally got out while waving the stick Becs had peed on all around the air between us. My friend, after finally coming out of her shocked stupor, snatched the test from my flailing hands and stepped back. Houston's eyes tracked that test like it might bite everyone in the room and he needed to be on alert for whatever might happen. That was about the time that Houston finally clued in to what was really going on.

"Is it Austin's?" He asked. Becs looked at him for a full minute before crumpling right there in front of us. "Dammit," Houston hissed.

"Don't tell him," Becs pleaded from her spot on my kitchen floor.

"Don't ask me to keep something like that a secret," he told her.

"I'll tell him, but…"

"Tell him. Decide what you're going to do together, but Becs, do it soon because I won't lie or keep it from him. He deserves to know."

"A part of me wants to argue with you about that." It hurt my heart to watch this woman, who was like a sister to me, crying over the asshole who had burned her twice before. Now, she would have a permanent reminder of him, whether he wanted anything to do with his child or not. It would be awful to have to watch her share a child with Jordan, because that's what it looked like might be the result of Austin's careless behavior.

Houston got down on the floor beside my best friend, pulled her into his lap, and cradled her there while she cried. If I could have married the man on the spot, I would have.

"I'm sorry he has his head so far up his ass, Becs. I don't know what to say about him. For years, his ass was grumpy because he gave you up."

"Yeah, he looked real grumpy after he ghosted me yet again after sex, only to see him kissing all over Jordan a couple days later. He was really torn up," she got out while wiping her snotty nose on Houston's shirt.

I wrinkled my nose up and went to go get a spare shirt that he had left behind on one of his stays. By the time I got back, Becs had her phone out and she was dialing.

"I'm going to put it on speakerphone, because I need you guys to be here for me." She glanced up into Houston's eyes, to get his permission. I understood why. He was Austin's brother. Technically, Houston should have been there for Austin, not Becs. When he nodded, she dialed and then waited as it kicked over to voicemail.

Then she sent a text. "I need to speak to you. It's important, please call immediately." She said out loud as she typed the message and hit send.

"Well, he's seen it." She flipped the phone around so we could all see that the message had been read, but no response came and no calls either.

Houston pulled his own phone and texted Austin to see what he was doing. The response was immediate. He was trying to fix things because Jordan was threatening to leave the bar and go work somewhere else, since she'd just seen Becs trying to call and text him.

Houston moved Becs off his lap so he could stand up. It was clear he was growing more agitated with his brother's bullshit.

"What?" Austin barked into the phone loud enough for all of us to hear him. "It's my fucking brother, lay off for a minute, J."

"You need to come to Clea's place, right now."

"I can't fucking leave."

"Get Dallas over there. Put me on speaker." He waited a minute to hear that Austin had done it before speaking again. "Jordan?" He called out.

"Yeah?" She answered.

"Shit or get off the pot, girl. I'm your boss too and I'm not playing the emotional blackmail games you keep using to keep Austin dangling by your strings. If you don't want to work at the bar, get a new fucking job. Try this bullshit again, and you'll need to look for another job anyway, because I'm sick of it. I will have you replaced if you don't want to work and just want another way to control my brother."

"What the fuck, Houston?" Austin yelled into the phone.

"I should be asking you, 'what the fuck' Austin. That is our bar. Our business. Stop bringing your personal shit there to fuck things up. If Jordan can't be a grown up about working with you when she's your fuck buddy, then she needs to find a new job. And you need to stop sleeping with employees. Now, get Dallas to cover for you, and get your ass over here. It's fucking important!"

Becs cringed at the way Houston was speaking to his brother. If for no other reason than the one I was worried about. Austin was going to be pissed when he showed up. That wasn't exactly the kind of mood you wanted a reluctant baby daddy to be in when you dropped the news on him.

About fifteen minutes later, Austin showed up. The minute I opened the door and he saw Becs scrunched into the corner of my couch, he started to turn around and leave. Then, I guess it hit him that she was crying, and he did a double-take and moved into the house.

"What's going on here?" He finally asked.

Becs didn't even bother to move from her spot. Instead, my beautiful best friend threw the positive pregnancy test at him. "That's what's going on."

The test had bounced off his chest and fell to the floor, but Austin reached down to pick it up and when he got a good look, his eyes immediately went comically wide. I watched as he stood there and shook his head, as if the gesture could erase what he saw with his own two eyes. "No." He growled. "You're saying this is mine?" If I hadn't just told my boyfriend I would marry him, I might have kicked his brother's ass because of the accusation in his tone.

Becs shook her head, as if to deny the truth of things, but Houston wouldn't let her. "I heard what you told Clea. He's the only person you've been with in six months. Don't lie to him now just because he's being a dick."

"What the fuck?" Austin asked his brother. Houston ignored him.

"I'm keeping it." Becs said. She stood from where she had been huddled up with her feelings on my couch, and got right in Austin's face. "This is MY baby. I don't want a thing from you, but your brother was right, you deserved to at least know. So, now you do, and you can go back to your far more important Jordan drama, just like you always do."

"I think this," he waved the stick around, and I cringed, thinking about possible pee particles flying about. "This just proved that bullshit needs to come to an end. We'll go get married, and…"

"No, we will not be getting married."

"You're having my kid, we're getting married," Austin demanded. I supposed that was the one time he and his brother had the same response.

"I refuse to marry you," Becs insisted.

"What? Why?"

"Look at you!" She shouted at him as Houston came over and wrapped his arms around me. Neither of us planned to leave the room though, because the situation was just a little bit volatile and I honestly feared for Austin's life if he kept pushing my obviously hormonal friend.

"You're still playing fuck buddies with the girl you promised to marry if you were both still single at thirty."

Houston looked down at me, as if to ask if I had spilled the beans about that. I shook my head, no. Letting him know that I would never tell her that. Granted, I also hadn't told him that she already knew, because Jordan had paid her a visit years ago. That was Becs' business.

"What the fuck? How did you even know about that?"

"You think Jordan didn't come to gloat after you ghosted me?"

"Are you serious?" He asked as venom dripped from his words.

"It doesn't matter. You chose her then. You chose her this last time too. I am very clearly not your choice, and never have been, so go live the life you promised her when you were ten years old. I'll live mine, and you don't have to be bothered with us."

"Jesus," Houston sighed and shook his head at his brother. "I told you that hole you were digging with Jordan was going to bury you one day." Houston let his arms drop from around me and he walked back toward my bedroom to get away from the scene before us. I followed because it felt like Becs needed privacy for her goodbye to the man who she once loved, the man who fathered her child, and proved too many times that he didn't love her enough to hang on.

When we got to my room, Houston spun me to face him. "Don't think I forgot that you agreed to marry me."

"You caught me by surprise," I argued, though if I were being honest, it didn't bother me the way it probably should have.

"No take backs," he insisted.

"I'm not the one that's pregnant though."

"I like Becs just fine, sweet Clea, but I'm not marrying her." He winked at me to let me know it was a joke.

"Okay, let me rephrase, you asked because you thought I was the one who was pregnant. I'm not. So, there's no need for you to do the right thing here."

He shrugged. "So, I still would have asked you eventually."

"Eventually, maybe. We're still very new, Houston."

"Sometimes, when you know, you know."

"You're serious?"

"Deadly."

I grinned widely at the man before I jumped right up into his arms, wrapped my legs around his waist and thrilled at the fact that he held me there in his strong arms with no inclination to let me go. I giggled as he dug his fingers into the fleshy part of my ass, before I leaned in to kiss the man I had been falling in love with. I only wished my best friend had been given the same response.

As if reading my mind, Houston shushed me and added his two cents. "Let's tone down our happy just for today," he suggested while tipping his head in the direction of my living room where we had left Becs and Austin to sort their shit.

"I don't hear anything." I told him, unable to hide the worry in my tone at the fact that there were no longer voices murmuring in the background.

Houston set me down on my feet and opened the bedroom door. I followed behind as he made his way back out to the living room where Austin sat with his elbows planted on his knees and his head hung into his hands.

"Aus?" Houston questioned.

"She left."

"Imagine that," I huffed out.

Austin lifted his head and glared at me for a moment before he straightened further and admitted, "I deserved that."

"No, you deserved worse for what you did."

"You're right, but I don't deserve to not be a part of my child's life."

"Becs would never do that. All she did was give you the out she thought you would want, since you proved to be such a coward multiple times already," I snapped. I'd be damned if he was going to paint her as the monster here.

"Clea!" Houston groused.

"No, she's right. I am a fucking coward. I didn't know how to deal with the pressure from Jordan. We have fun together, but I know in my heart that she's not the one."

"How would you know that?" Houston prodded, an obvious agenda to his questioning. It made me pay closer attention.

"Because I know who is, but I already screwed everything up."

"Surely, you are not talking about my best friend!" The shock in my voice had to be evident. If this man ever thought she was the one, he was wrong, he didn't just fuck up. He made damn sure that he would never get her again.

Austin stood and stared down at me, as if it was a crime to doubt him. I laughed, even though there was nothing humorous about the situation.

"If that's the case, then why in the hell did you run out on her after sex, and then ghost her again? If she was the one, why were you sucking face with your fuck buddy in the theater just days after sleeping with my best friend again like that never happened. Why in the hell, when my bestie gave you a second chance, would you throw it all away again?"

"Because when Jordan showed up that night, after Becs left, it was to tell me she's pregnant," Austin yelled at me.

"Holy shit! You stupid fuck!" Houston stated rather pointedly to his brother.

I just stood there, trying to process that information. "Did you tell her that?"

"No, she left before I could explain."

I sank down into the space Austin had vacated moments ago on my couch. My eyes never left Austin's. It was almost as if I was challenging him to take it all back and make what he'd just revealed untrue. What a mess.

"Becs is going to be devastated all over again." I shook my head at him in disappointment again before shifting my gaze to the floor beside my feet. "Do me a favor, and let me know when you plan on filling her in, because I'd like to make sure that I'm there for her. She's going to need someone by her side who actually cares about what this will mean and how devastated she will be.

"I do fucking care!"

"Yeah? Well, you have a shitty way of showing it. You could have just told her the truth before dipping out of her life and attempting to ghost her again. Jesus, you ran skipping off to start a family with your fuck buddy like Becs didn't even matter, and you claim to care? She deserved to at least hear the truth from you."

"I fucking know!" Austin yelled as he started pacing the room.

"Calm that shit down, brother." Houston warned while putting himself between his brother and me.

"Christ, Houston, I'm not going to attack your girlfriend."

"Fiancé," Houston corrected.

"What?" Austin looked down at Clea's empty ring finger, as if to get confirmation of what his brother just said.

"I asked her to marry me, and she said, 'Yes'. I didn't have a ring because it wasn't planned yet."

"You thought the pregnancy test was hers?" His brother surmised.

"I did, but that changes nothing."

"You know what? I'm not even going to tell you to pump the brakes. One of us needs to be decisive about our lives instead of fucking them all to hell for idiotic reasons."

"I agree," Houston said as he pulled me to my feet to stand beside him. "You should probably go fill Mom and Dad in on what you have going on in your life before they hear it through the grapevine somehow, and you know they will. Jordan is all right, but I don't see her keeping her mouth shut if she thinks she finally got you collared."

"What's that supposed to mean?"

"You've been stringing that poor girl along since you were kids. She's done everything in her power to make sure she ends up with you in the end, and you have done nothing but give her reasons to keep her hopes up while you went out to explore your options. She's not letting go now that she has her claws sunk in and you're down to the wire on hitting thirty soon. How do you think she's going to react to you having another baby on the way with someone else, especially when that someone else is Becs – the one woman you actually shut her down for in the past?"

"I don't know, man."

The sheer desolation on Austin's face almost made me feel bad for him. Almost. Then I remembered that he fucked my best friend over, all on his own, and I told my empathy to fuck off this time. Houston wasn't done counseling his brother though, and since he had his arms wrapped around me again, I had to stand there and hear this out to the end.

"I'm assuming since Jordan threatened to quit at the bar, that you still haven't made any promises to her?" Houston asked.

"No, I haven't, beyond letting her know that I would be there for the baby."

"She's going to keep pushing for the marriage bit that you

offered Becs today. Shit, man, what do you think is going to happen when Jordan finds out you offered to marry Becs on the spot when you didn't do that for her?"

"I don't fucking know, Houston. Everything is a damn mess."

"First thing, you need to find out when both women have an appointment to confirm their pregnancies with a doctor. You show up to both of those appointments and make damn sure there are actually pregnancies involved before you make any more decisions."

My surprised gasp caught Houston's attention and caused him to tighten his hold on me. "I'm not saying she lied. Obviously, you were here with her when she took the test, but they have been known to be wrong sometimes, and she only took one, right?"

"Yeah, that's true," I conceded.

"Okay," Houston said, as he turned his attention back to his brother, "so demand to be there for the doctor appointments to verify they're both pregnant. Then, we'll make a plan. You're not in this alone."

Houston let me go and had a brief, whispered conversation with his brother before Austin finally left my house and the two of us were finally alone.

"I'm honestly super glad that I'm not pregnant too after all that."

Houston chuckled. "You and me both. I would have been happy to raise a baby with you, don't get me wrong, but I think it will be better if we get some time just as husband and wife before we add a baby to the mix."

"It's so weird to talk about that," I mumbled.

"What? Getting married? Babies?"

"Both. Everyone is going to think I'm crazy or that I was cheating on Jeff too."

"Nah. They'll know what we tell them, that we were fated to

be together and that we're done wasting time after so much was stolen from us."

"You really feel that?"

"Yeah, my sweet girl, I do."

I sighed contentedly and leaned into Houston who picked me up and carried me back to the bedroom. He dropped me there before running back to secure the house and lock up, but then my man came and destroyed me in the physical sense only to put me back together, and do it all over again with his mouth, his fingers, and that big, beautiful cock of his.

Yeah, there was no denying it. I would marry this man tomorrow if he asked me to. I'd marry him over again, every single day for the rest of our lives, if it meant being that blissed out in his arms forever.

11

My bestie refused to even acknowledge Austin's demand to be at her doctor appointment, so instead she took me. She also gave me permission to take a photo of the sonogram of the little bean she has inside her. To me it just looked like a tiny little blob of ink, but Becs was assured the blob was her baby.

So, there I was with lunch in hand for my boyfriend, or was he my fiancé now? It was still so weird to me that he had proposed on the spot and I had accepted without really needing to think. I picked up some deli sandwiches, drinks, and chips from the place down the block that had never been known to give people random, explosive diarrhea. No, I was not taking my chances on new places that popped up in the mall again.

I also didn't have to take my chances with meeting Houston's entire family for Sunday dinner – yet! That was on account of Austin's baby drama taking precedence.

So, imagine my surprise, when I walked into Houston's office with lunch, and a sonogram image for his brother, only to find his ex-fiancé draped over his desk with her blouse practically hanging all the way open and her tits wagging hello to the man in question. It took a few seconds for my eyes to move and note the fact that Houston was eyeball deep in some report or other on his desk and hadn't been paying the woman the least bit of attention. Good boy! Still, something needed to be done about the shark, and I hoped he would man up and do it without me needing to say anything. For once, I needed for someone to have their own shit together.

Even though I noticed that Houston wasn't paying attention to Samantha, I still got mad enough to throw our lunch on his desk and turn around to leave. Hey, I'm a woman who has been scorned, and recently. Sometimes, we just really need a minute to collect ourselves.

"Clea? Wait a minute, where are you going?" Houston called out. I turned to see him finally notice his ex-fiancé standing there with her tits hanging out of her shirt.

"Samantha? What the fuck do you think you're doing? Get out!"

The woman had the nerve to stomp her foot, which sent her boobs fluttering in the barely there bra she had on. Yes, it was visible because, yes, her tits really were just hanging out there. She had the buttons on her blouse undone down to practically her navel.

"We are at work, Houston! That woman is the one who needs to leave." She had the audacity to point at me, which only highlighted the fact that her tits were still hanging out in a wholly unprofessional manner while she was at work.

Houston looked fit to be tied. His face had turned red, and his fists were clenched at his sides before he knuckled down on the desk and leaned over far enough to get in her face, but not quite far enough to have her displayed tits reach out and touch any part of him.

"I don't know what the fuck you thought you were doing coming into my office looking like that, but this will damn sure be the last time it ever happens."

"Houston," she pouted.

"No. Get out. Go get some proper work clothes on, and then you can finish out the next two weeks. Start looking for employment elsewhere. I'm not doing this anymore."

Samantha stood there with mouth agape, stunned by the fact that Houston had just fired her. Honestly, aside from the fact that my own tits were still well-ensconced in my bra and shirt, I probably mirrored her shocked expression.

"Sorry, sweet Clea, I didn't even notice what she was wearing. I was lost in this file and hadn't taken my eyes off it until you dropped something on my desk."

"Lunch," I managed to say. "I came by to have lunch with you."

"Yet you were going to drop it and run?" He asked while quirking a brow to emphasize his question.

I shrugged, but it was Samantha who spoke. "What do you mean, you didn't notice? My breasts, which you used to love playing with, were right there in your face!"

"Well, they weren't enough to get my attention," Houston told her as he shrugged. "Now, since you just admitted to trying to pull more shit while on the job, you can forget the two-week's notice and just pack your shit up and go."

"I have a child to feed, Houston! You can't just fire me like that."

"I can and I just did. You have been on notice for a while now because of your behavior. You know you have a child to take care of, it was your decision to act right and keep your job or keep pulling this shit and lose it. Your choice. What you do to keep a roof over your child's head is on you. It's not my kid."

Samantha stormed past me after that. If she hadn't been trying to put the moves on my man while he was working, I might have felt sorry for her. Houston was right though; she made her decisions knowing exactly what was at stake.

"You didn't have to fire her. I knew nothing was going on. I just couldn't deal with being in the same room with her like that."

"And that is why she's gone. I hope this won't be the only time that you come to share lunch with me. I won't work in an environment where you feel uncomfortable coming here to surprise me. I'm just sorry that I didn't see what she was up to before you walked in. She was babbling away and I tuned her out because I had something far more interesting to hold my attention."

"Something bad?"

"What?"

"In the file," I nodded to the thing that held him in rapture when I came in to bring him food. "Was it something bad?"

"No. Just," he sighed and then his eyes met mine again. "I had a private investigator look into Jordan."

"What?" I asked, eyes wide and shock clearly written on my face. "Jordan has been a friend of Austin's since childhood, right? I would think you guys know everything there is to know about her life."

"There were some things that didn't add up.

"What things?"

"After the whole big blowup at your apartment last week, I remembered something about her having issues years ago. Sunday, when I sat down with Austin to tell my parents about what's going on, my mom sort of confirmed what I thought I'd overheard then. Jordan had a bunch of issues years ago."

"Okay?"

"My mom was talking to hers about how it would be really difficult, if not impossible, for her to get pregnant way back then."

I cut him off there because I could see where this might be going. "Houston, sometimes women get that kind of diagnosis and they end up being the lucky ones, or the diagnosis was incorrect."

Houston slid the file over to me. I glanced down and saw paperwork stating that she had been given a partial hysterectomy. No more uterus meant zero chance of a viable pregnancy.

"No one would be this cruel to another person, would they?" I asked, unable to believe a woman who couldn't have children would try to trap a man with a fake baby. A man who had been her life-long best friend definitely didn't deserve that, no matter how idiotic he had been to mix sex with their friendship.

"She's desperate," Houston reminded me.

"Yeah, but how is she planning to explain it?"

Houston shrugged. "Who knows. She'd probably tell him she lost the baby and maybe throw her uterus into the mix as a result so the guilt of her never being able to do it in the future would rest on his shoulders."

"That's awful!" I cried.

"It was a crazy plan from the beginning, no matter how she meant to carry it out. I still can't believe she would go this far. I've always liked Jordan, even if I did think she was all wrong for my brother." Houston shook his head, as if trying to rattle his brain so things would make sense somehow.

"I brought this with me today too," I told him as I slid the sonogram image over the desk. "I thought Austin would want the proof, and now I see that he's going to need it. Do you mind if I tell Becs about the Jordan situation?"

"That's not her business, Clea."

"Isn't it?" I asked, worried for my friend. "You don't think Austin is going to go a little crazy that his best friend perpetrated this huge lie and take that out on my best friend too? You don't think he'll get in her face about whether or not her pregnancy is real too?"

"Shit. I hadn't thought about that."

"I'm glad I did. Please, say you're okay with this, because Houston, even if you aren't, she needs to know."

He nodded and we both stared down at the sonogram image of Becs' little bean sitting next to the folder that called Jordan out as a liar. It was a lie that ruined everything for Becs and Austin getting back together and even though she would be under-standing about the woman putting him in that position, my best friend would never forgive him. He had the chance to tell her about Jordan's claim and why he chose her, but he had tucked his head in the sand instead. What a mess.

"Jordan must really love him," I muttered.

"No, she doesn't." when I looked askance of him, Houston explained. "If she really loved him, she would let him be happy and not run these kinds of games on him. Every time my brother has pulled away and attempted to have a life outside of her little bubble, she has pulled some stunt or other to win his affections back to her again.

"Are you going to tell him?"

"I was trying to figure out how to do that," Houston admitted.

"No need," Austin said. I turned to see him standing in the doorway of Houston's office. "I just came from Mom explaining things to me, and how it might not be possible, but you just filled in the blanks she was missing. Mom didn't know about the hysterectomy." He moved over to sit in the chair beside mine. "How in the hell did she think she would get away with this farce?"

"Maybe she didn't realize that her mom told ours. Lydia has been gone a couple years now." Austin looked devastated, but I don't think what Houston just added to the picture was the reason. "I can't believe she would stoop this low."

Houston and I both stayed quiet and watched Austin as he attempted to come to terms with the news.

"You did though," he added after pointing to the open folder on the desk. "You said she's pulled something every time we started drifting apart, and you're right. I just never saw it. How fucking stupid have I been?"

"In her defense, I think she's been infatuated with you so long that she was having a hard time letting go, and then not letting go became a habit," I explained.

"You're defending her?" Austin growled.

"Not at all. I'm just telling you what was probably going on with her." I sighed. "Women who are in love will sometimes lie to themselves more than anyone else, and then do whatever it takes to try to make that lie a reality. You need to be firm with her about what you want, but you also need to be fair because she might have gone completely overboard, but something in your interactions made her believe that was…"

"You think something I did made it seem okay for her to fake a pregnancy?" He asked indignantly.

"Not okay. Doing that is never okay. What I'm saying is that something about your prior interactions led her to believe that everything would play out all right and that she would still have you in the end. Becs mentioned something about the two of you getting married when you are thirty, if you haven't found someone else." I explained. He still looked clueless, so I laid it out for him.

"You have been keeping Jordan on a string as your fallback plan. You were always her first option. When you never took that marriage pact off the table, she worked to do whatever she had to, to keep it there. She's the one who told Becs about it to get her to back off."

"We made that stupid marriage shit up when we were kids," Austin argued. "The last time I think we even talked about it, we were thirteen."

"Does she bring it up sometimes?"

"Yeah, but only as a joke. We haven't ever talked about it in a serious way in our adult lives."

"It might not have been serious to you, but she held onto that childhood promise as her life goal. Every time you pulled away, she did her best to reel you back in. You're getting closer to the goal line, Becs being back in the picture meant that she was beyond desperate. Think about it. Be firm, but try to remember not to be too harsh because you're the one that has been dangling her from that string. Whether you thought about the marriage pact or not, you kept going back there as a fuck buddy when things didn't work out. You had to realize that she expected you would stay eventually."

"Fuck!" Austin breathed out before collapsing back in the chair, and he looked absolutely defeated.

"Now that you understand what you're working with, maybe you can clear it up with Becs and..."

I cut Houston off, despite the fact that he was trying to give his brother some hope. I wouldn't allow it to be false hope that would end up crushing my best friend's spirit even more.

"No. You won't be able to get through to Becs like that. She knew about the marriage thing. Jordan filled her in about that years ago. Becs won't trust you or Jordan after everything that happened."

"What in the hell am I supposed to do then?"

"Give her time. Let her see how serious you are. Make things clear with Jordan and put that situation to rights before you ever attempt to approach Becs, because if it is still an unresolved issue, she will continue to not trust anything you say or do."

Austin stood, ready to leave until something on the desk caught his attention. "What is this? I thought you said Jordan couldn't have a baby?"

"I brought that with me today," I told him quickly before he could make any further wrong assumptions.

"This is..." Austin glanced up from the image of his baby and pierced me with his fierce gaze. "You went with her?"

"I did, and she told me I could bring that back for you."

"She wouldn't let me go to see my own kid, but she took you to be the middleman?"

"Austin, stop and think about what you've put her through. Do you blame her?"

His shoulders began to shake as the emotions he'd been hiding behind his angry facade started to spill over. Tears fell down his face in torrents. "If Jordan hadn't said she was pregnant, I would have never left Becs. We would be together and I could have been with her finding out about our baby together."

Houston and I were both stunned silent as Austin threw his head back and bellowed out the worst, animalistic sound I'd ever heard. I hoped to never hear its like again, because it was the sound of total devastation.

Not long after that, Austin took off with both the file and the sonogram image. It was obvious he went to confront Jordan with what she had cost him and most likely herself too. I didn't see any room for Jordan in Austin's life after what had been done.

"Well, this has been the worst lunch date I've ever had. The only way to top that would have been to have someone fall over dead on my desk," Houston said in an effort to bring some light to the situation. Then he thought better of it. "Let's not tempt fate. Please, don't fall over dead on my desk."

"You either," I told him as both of our gazes landed on the sandwiches that I had brought in earlier.

"Maybe we should try dinner?" He suggested.

"I could be convinced. We should probably do it at either your place or mine, so we don't accidentally run into drama anywhere. It seems to be the day for it."

Houston chuckled at that. "I love my brother, but he certainly landed himself right in the middle of a giant shitstorm."

"I hope he manages to pull his head out of his ass long enough to do right by my friend," I added. "But, what's between them is between them. I just want you to know that I won't hold it against you when they're fighting like cats and dogs."

"That goes both ways, sweet Clea."

"Good. See you tonight?" I asked as I stood to leave and head back to my own job.

"Pack a bag and meet me at my place around seven."

"Okay."

"And Clea?"

"Yeah?"

"My mom still wants to meet you, so we need to go ring shopping before Sunday."

"Oh my God!" I yelped as I ran from his office. "We said no more drama today!"

I slowed my pace to a walk once I got to his door, but only because listening to my man's laughter sent little zings of pleasure through my body.

12

IT TOOK A BLOW JOB, SOME ANAL PLAY, AND ABOUT TWELVE orgasms to convince Houston that we should put off the ring shopping and allow me to meet his family as his girlfriend before we dropped the engagement bomb on them.

"You look nervous," the foolish man in the car beside me said.

I turned to stare at him, even though he could only see me out of his peripheral, the grin on his handsome face grew in size. "I am meeting your entire family today. One mom, one dad, two sisters, and…"

"You've already met my brothers, so that takes some of the stress off."

"Men!" I threw up my hands as if I was fed up with the jerk. Truth be told, I was equally excited to meet the women of the Mercer family. They must have done something right to produce at least one good male in the bunch.

"They'll love you, Clea."

"How do you know that?"

"Because I love you," he said, as if it wasn't the first time he actually verbalized that to me. We were engaged, and it just occurred to me that we hadn't even swapped I love yous yet.

When I didn't say anything because I was too busy working through that conundrum, he spoke again. "Since I love you, they kind of have to."

"You should probably pull the car over," I insisted.

"What? Why?"

"Because you can't just tell me you love me for the first time and not expect me to jump your bones."

"It wasn't the first time," he argued.

"Yeah, it was."

"No," he continued to argue, but it was clear he was sifting through his memories to find another time he might have said it. "Well, damn. I've said it in my head so many times, it just felt natural, I guess."

"I love you too," I admitted, although somewhat shyly.

"Now, I really should pull the car over, but we're here, so, it was inevitable," he teased.

"We can't jump each other's bones on your parents' front lawn."

"Says who?" Houston laughed as he said it so I hoped that he was joking. Making out on my future in-laws' front lawn prior to meeting them would certainly be one way to break the ice. Probably the wrong way. "Stay put," he insisted, interrupting my oddball thoughts.

"Yes, sir."

Houston's sexy, low growl set me tingling in all the worst places when I had to meet his family. I turned to watch my handsome man round the front of the car and noticed that his parents were already standing on the porch watching. Once he opened my door and helped me out, I decided to go for broke and break the ice the best way possible, with humor.

"Don't believe it!" I called out to the couple standing on the porch. "This is the first time he's ever been a gentleman to me, it's all for show."

"What the hell, Clea?" Houston shouted in shock over my lie.

He was truly stunned until he heard both his parents cackling from their spot as guardians to the front door. "You're going to pay for that later."

I beamed a brilliant smile his way and he took full advantage by leaning down and planting a wanton kiss on my mouth in full view of God and everyone. I couldn't bring myself to mind though.

"Mom and Dad don't need to see their other son actually impregnate a chick. Save it for the bedroom, asshole." I rolled my eyes as Houston pulled away from me and flipped his younger brother off.

"Hello, Dallas. Good to see you out of your diaper," I called out to him. The man turned red as his mother had questions.

"Why has Houston's poor girlfriend seen you in a diaper? Dammit, Dallas, I didn't raise a delinquent."

"Good job," Houston whispered to me as we walked toward the house. "Feeling better?"

I didn't get the chance to answer because I was immediately swallowed up in a hug from Houston's father. "You have a good attitude with my boys, it will serve you well in the future."

"You raised some pretty fine boys," I told him truthfully. Yes, Dallas was an insufferable asshole, but he came to our rescue when he didn't have to on that awful food poisoning night. Austin had his good side, even if his love life was a huge mess thanks to his loyalty and misguided ways with his childhood best friend.

"Come on in," Mr. Mercer invited me.

"Not so fast," Houston's mom called out before we could move past where she had been trying to suss out the diaper issues her youngest boy had. I giggled again when I heard her say, "Diapers? Really, Dallas?"

"Hello, Mrs. Mercer. It's good to meet you."

"You too sweetheart," she offered before pulling me into a hug just as big as her husband had given me.

"Thank you again for the soup," I whispered in her ear.

"You're welcome, honey. From what I hear, your night was bad enough without my boy trying to feed you something from a can." There was a twinkle in her eye that made my face redden in embarrassment. Yeah, Dallas had evidently told her the whole sordid story.

"My poor pants," I lamented, which made both of us crack up.

"Come on, let's get you inside to meet the girls. They've been dying to find out who has taken all of their brother's attention."

"All I'm saying is how do you know she's not lying about having your kid too? You burned the girl before, maybe this is her revenge, trying to pin an unwanted pregnancy on you," a woman was asking Austin when we walked in.

That was my best friend she was bad mouthing, but I wasn't sure if it was wise for me to interrupt, considering it was the first time meeting these people. My anxiety started to spike when Houston spoke up for me. Well, for Becs.

"Victoria, that's enough!"

"What? It's not like you haven't thought the same thing." When she took another look at his angry face she still doubled down. "You must have. We all have."

"No, I haven't because I know Becs. She wouldn't do that."

"That's what we all thought about Jordan too," Victoria insisted.

"Not really," another woman muttered.

"I'm with Katy on that one," Dallas added. "Never did like Jordan all that much."

"Me either," Katy added. "She always had a weird glint in her eye when Aus was around."

"Okay, well just because you guys suspected Jordan was up to something doesn't mean this other girl isn't up to worse."

"She's my best friend," I jumped in, and everyone grew quiet. "Becs is my very best friend and has been for years. She was in love with your brother and absolutely destroyed when he ghosted her all those years ago. Against her better judgement, she thought he had grown up and chose to give him a second chance, only to have him do the same thing to her all over again. Trust me when I say, had Houston not been there to see that test, Austin wouldn't even know about the baby yet. Not that she wouldn't have told him, but that she would have chosen to work through all the possible scenarios first to find the best way to deal with him if he ghosted out on both of them, if he wanted to be a part of the baby's life and she was forced to co-parent. What Becs would never do is fake a pregnancy and manipulate someone into loving her when they don't want to."

A startled cry rang out from behind me, and I turned to see Jordan standing there with tears flowing down her cheeks. Why she was here was beyond me and apparently everyone else too.

"What are you doing here?" Austin yelled at her.

"I came to apologize. To everyone," she sniffled. "I don't know why I did it. I was so angry with you when I found out you were with Becs that night. I didn't know what else would keep you away from her. I just knew I had to, otherwise I'd lose you."

"Well, good job, you made sure to lose me anyway."

"I didn't know she was pregnant for real. Why didn't you tell me?'

"It's none of your damn business, Jordan. We can't even be friends now because of what you did. Why the hell would I tell you that you ruined any chance of me being able to have a healthy relationship with my baby's mother?"

"Oh my God!" The woman cried out. "I'm so sorry, Aus. What can I do? I can talk to her, explain things."

"You will stay the hell away from her and while you're at it, you can stay away from me and my family too."

"Austin," his mother chided softly.

"No, Mom. She ruins things. Her selfishness ruined everything."

"Oh, it helped things along, but you are the reason things

were ruined, my boy. Don't put all that weight on Jordan's shoulders. She did wrong, but so did you."

Austin had the presence of mind to look shame-faced as his father escorted an openly weeping Jordan out of the house. "Let's get you back home, honey."

"Don't hate him for caring for her," Mrs. Mercer said to me. "She was my best friend's daughter. No matter what she's done, we still have to look out for her."

"I don't think ill of him. I admire you both for caring even when you're probably angry too."

"You got that right. She and Austin both deserve to be taken over someone's knee and paddled until they learn their lesson."

I tried to suppress my giggles at the thought of this tiny woman putting Austin's large frame over her knee. It didn't work and Mrs. Mercer ended up taking a swat at me instead. "Stop that. The mental imagery is a bit off, I'll give you that," she finally said to break the tension.

"Now, girls," Mrs. Mercer called out. "Come meet your Houston's girlfriend."

Both of the women who had been arguing over what Jordan might or might not be capable of made their way toward their mother and me. "This is my oldest," Houston's mom said. "Victoria, meet Clea."

"Clea? What's that short for?" I wasn't sure if I liked Victoria. She seemed to have an attitude with me since I wasn't afraid to speak up for Becs. Maybe, she saw me in the same light that she tried to paint my best friend.

"Don't mind her," the younger woman said. "I'm Katy, and the youngest of this crazy bunch."

"It's nice to meet you," I told her before turning back to her older sister. "My name is Clea. That's it, just Clea."

"Why?"

"Because my mother was loopy on the good drugs after having me and her nurse was an asshole," I cringed and looked back toward Mrs. Mercer, who was grinning. "Pardon my language."

She waved it off as if it were nothing.

"Anyway, my mom wanted to name me Cleopatra, but all she managed to get out was Cleo, and since she was high as a kite and southern as could be, it sounded to the nurse more like Clea. So, the nurse wrote it down that way, had my mother sign the paper, and that's how I got my name."

"And a lovely story to tell nosy people along with it," Mrs. Mercer chimed in, much to everyone's amusement except Victoria's.

"Seriously, don't mind her. She had a run-in with a very bad ex-best friend the other day and she's back to thinking everyone is out to get everyone else. She'll get over it again, eventually." Katy sounded hopeful, but the look she tossed back at her sister said that hope was probably dead and her older sister was too jaded to ever approach relationships in a good way again.

Victoria scoffed at her sister then looked me dead in the eye. "Don't hurt my brother." It felt like a warning had been issued, but I had no problem with it because I felt the same about Houston. If someone hurt him, they would have to deal with me. I didn't bother with a verbal response. Instead, I followed the women into the kitchen with Houston hot on my heels.

"So, what does your mother do, Clea?"

"No clue," I answered honestly. When everyone's attention came back to me, I realized my life story was going to be put out there for all of them. "Lulu, my mom, left shortly after I was born. My father was away in the military and didn't make it back for the birth, so my Granna Sabra took me in. My dad said he couldn't afford a kid without the military benefits, so Granna kept me while Dad went off on his missions and was stationed in different places. I see him a few times a year, more now that he has retired."

"That sucks," Katy called out.

"Katy!" Mrs. Mercer admonished.

"What? It does."

"It's okay. I'm sure it sounds bad enough to people who grew up in a big family like yours, but my life wasn't so bad, I love my Granna and she was definitely the better choice to raise me. Lulu would have dragged me all over the country and back and probably would have forgotten me somewhere along the way. My dad was always on the go, being sent off places at a moment's notice. My Granna though, she taught me everything I know about my business and more. She's the reason I was so successful starting out."

"Well, that's good that you had someone who was stable and gave you a good foundation in life," Mrs. Mercer told me. "Normally, we would wait for Jacob to get back, but I have a feeling he will be a while getting Jordan settled."

"I think I should go," Austin chimed in. I noticed him watching me as he said it. If he was looking for my permission, he wouldn't get it. As far as I was concerned, he had burned the bridges with my friend and should only hope that she allowed him to co-parent with her. When I said nothing, his shoulders drooped.

"You don't see your friend forgiving my boy, do you?" Mrs. Mercer asked quietly.

I shook my head. "If it had been the first time he messed up like that and chose Jordan over her, then she might have given him the benefit of the doubt. If he had at least talked to her and told Becs that Jordan claimed she was pregnant, she would have still been heartbroken, but she would have understood. Instead, he just dropped her and cut off all communication."

"I didn't know what to do," he said.

"Let me ask you this, Austin. If you were the one having Becs' baby and she had been so careless and heartless with you, would you trust that person to be in your life or your baby's life? Or would you go into protection mode and try to do damage control early on? Becs' biggest fear is that you are going to demand to be involved with her child and then when push comes to shove, you're just going to bolt. She can handle being left high and dry herself, but she would never put her child in a position to feel that kind of hurt and abandonment."

"I would never do that to my kid. It's why I fucking chose Jordan to begin with. I thought I had to pick my kid above what I wanted."

"Well, you should have been man enough to let her know that's what you were doing from the beginning."

Austin slumped into a chair that was a few seats down the table from mine. "She'll come around man," Dallas told him as he held onto his shoulder.

"Would she be willing to meet with me, do you think?" Mrs. Mercer asked.

"I don't see why not."

"Good. After dinner, we'll go see her then." My eyes grew round in surprise. "Unlike my son, I'm not one to wait around for things to make themselves right."

I hid the grin that bloomed on my face at her admonishment for Austin along with her forthrightness. Mrs. Mercer wasn't one to coddle her children, that was good to know.

"So, did Houston tell you guys his big news?" Dallas asked out of the blue.

I glanced at Houston who looked just as stumped as I was.

Dallas grinned maniacally. "Saw you ring shopping man," Dallas pointed out.

"Dallas Giles Mercer! How dare you ruin that surprise for your future sister-in-law!" Mrs. Mercer admonished.

"Hey, now! No need to three-name me, Mom. She already said yes to him."

Every set of eyes at the table turned toward my empty ring finger at that point, and I wished that the floor would swallow me up.

"So, where is it?" Houston's mom asked. "You're not trying to hide things from me, are you son?"

"We haven't picked a ring yet. I asked. She said 'Okay' and that was it."

"He walked in on Becs and Clea after they'd taken pregnancy tests and saw Becs' results," Austin supplied helpfully. My face had to look like an overripe tomato at that point because I could feel the furnace-worthy heat flaming my cheeks.

"I know we had the talk," Mrs. Mercer whispered to her son, but everyone heard her anyway. The room filled with laughter and all I could do was quietly plot my revenge against Dallas. He winked at me when I turned my attention to him, then his eyes slid to his sullen brother. The nod I offered in deference to why Houston and I had been thrown under the bus was all I could manage. Dallas was trying to get his brother out of the hot seat. I got it.

"I particularly remember the part where they're only ninety-eight percent effective. We had one break. Clea is not pregnant, but I still want very much to marry her."

"I thought you guys just started dating?" Katy asked.

"It's been a couple months," Houston corrected. I watched as his sister's eyebrows shot up into her hairline.

"Soulmates!" The reverent way the word rolled off her lips let me know the girl was not teasing, and the barely choked back laughter from Victoria proved she thought very differently. I brushed it off and left Victoria to her misery. If I hadn't been living with this relationship with Houston, I'd probably be skeptical too.

"Your father and I were married nine weeks after we met," Mrs. Mercer told the table full of her children.

"What?" Austin asked.

"No way!" Victoria piped up.

Houston just grinned at me, as if that wasn't news to him.

"When you know, you know." That was Mr. Mercer, who had

sneaked back in at some point and leaned in to plant a kiss on his wife's head. "Would have married her the first day, if she would have let me."

"How did we not know this?" Katy asked her parents, then she seemed to notice the shit-eating grin on her brother's face and turned her attention to him. "How did you know and the rest of us didn't?"

"Unlike some of my children," Mr. Mercer said as he glared around the table playfully. "Houston comes to me for advice and he's usually smart enough to take it."

"Besides," Houston directed at his sister, "Clea and I were fated to be together. We were set up on a blind date years ago, and if it hadn't been for our jackass brother, we would have been together all this time."

"You don't know that," Dallas pouted.

Houston turned to look at me, and the minute our eyes met, he said, "Yeah, I do."

I was completely speechless. The past six years of my romantic life suddenly seemed like such a waste. Then again, if I had been blissed out in the love that was promised with Houston, maybe I wouldn't have taken such careful time in building my business. Maybe, things happened the way they did for a reason, but that didn't mean I disagreed with Houston's assessment. If we had found one another then, we would have still been together and happy. Of that, I had no doubt.

13

Color me surprised when I started receiving texts from an unknown number.

Unknown Number: I miss you.

Unknown Number: What can I do to make things up to you?

Unknown Number: Darla's baby isn't mine. She had it and the test was done already.

I slid my phone over to Becs who rolled her eyes after reading the message. We both knew who it was. Jeff couldn't contact me with his old number because I blocked him early on after the whole catching him fucking my assistant over my desk.

Clea: And this matters to me, why?

Jeff's new number: It proves I'm not the father.

Clea: The fact that you needed DNA evidence of that still proves you were cheating on me even longer than I originally thought and with more people. What about Hillary's child? Or the other two? You are out of your damn mind. So, fuck off, Jeff.

I didn't wait for a response and just blocked his sorry ass. Again.

"What did he hope to gain from that?" Becs asked.

"Who knows? It's Jeff. He's probably still hoping to change his mother's mind about disinheriting him. She called me a couple of weeks ago to ask if there was any chance that I could forgive her son and still marry him."

"Are you serious?"

"Yeah. I told her that I hoped she enjoyed helping him change all those diapers because it would be a cold day in hell before I ever stepped up to that plate. I was lucky to escape that relationship without any diseases."

"So, what's going on with you and Houston?"

"I'm glad you asked, because it involves you too."

"Um, no offense, but I don't want to be a part of some contrived threesome, pregnancy fetish thing you guys have going on."

"What the..." I smacked my friend on the arm. "You're an idiot," I told her as we both laughed. "Actually, Houston asked me to move in with him."

"And live in sin again?" Becs asked with a mock gasp.

I rolled my eyes. "Yes, we plan to live in sin until the wedding. Anyway, the part you play in this was when we were trying to decide just whose house we would live in. Mine is paid for thanks to my aunt. He still has a mortgage. I was thinking though, we could live in his and that would free my place up to rent out to someone who will need more space in a few months."

Tears immediately welled up in Becs' eyes. "You're going to let me rent your house?"

"Sure am. You need more space than your tiny apartment provides. I'll keep your rent the same as what you're paying now and it can include the utilities. We'll call that my first baby shower gift."

"I can't ask you to do that. You could get twice as much rent for your place without throwing utilities in on top of it."

"You're not asking. I'm offering. The house was given to me free and clear, Becs. Let me give you a place to stay with your baby that you can afford. Being a single parent is going to be hard enough. Let me make it easier on you." She didn't look convinced, so I smiled at her and sank the last nail in the coffin that would make her agree. "Besides, you would be doing me a favor. I'd have someone at the house who I know will care for it. Houston hasn't said so, but I get the feeling that he doesn't want to move into mine because I shared the space with Jeff before. While I've tried to erase all memories of my ex from my brain, it would drive Houston crazy, wondering 'what if' all the time."

"Fine, but I'm only agreeing because if anything ever happens with you and Houston, there's plenty of room for you, me, and the baby."

"Hopefully, that never becomes a necessity, but on the bright side, it will mean that we only live two streets away. I can be there to help with the baby when you need a break."

"That'll be great. My parents aren't exactly happy with the news that I'm going to be a single parent. The disapproval and disappointment are awful. Like I don't already have a broken heart to deal with, or the fact that I'm going to be someone's mother and doing it alone. Suddenly, I have far more sympathy for the teen moms out there who go through this. I'm closing in on thirty and this shit is scary as hell."

"I know you probably don't want to hear this right now, but there is a whole family out there who wants to know you and would be there for the baby. I get that you hate Austin right now, but his family didn't do this to you. They didn't break your heart, so if you need to lean on them, maybe you should allow yourself that."

"What if they're just trying to be nice so they can help Austin steal my baby from me?"

I chuckled. "I have no clue what being hormonal does to the brain, but you sound so paranoid right now."

"I watched a Lifetime movie," she admitted in a low whisper.

"Are the green men listening in right now?" I whispered back.

"Oh, shut up!" Suddenly, my ornery friend didn't mind being loud and it made me laugh harder.

"You're the one getting ready to make tinfoil hats. Listen, I've met his family. While the older sister is a bit of a bitter Betty, the rest of them seem quite lovely. Dallas and Austin aside anyway. Austin's parents aren't exactly happy with the way he has handled things. I just think that maybe you could give them a chance, but of course, that is completely up to you to decide."

Becs sat there in contemplative silence for a bit. "I guess it would be best for the baby to know his or her extended family. I'm so scared, Clea. Like, all the time."

"I'm here for you. No matter what."

"I know. I just hate putting you in a position where one day you may have to pick a side."

"Never. That will never happen. Houston is pretty ticked off at his brother too, you know. Austin knows he fucked up. Everyone knows that Austin fucked up and that whether Jordan lied or not, he still didn't handle things like the adult he's supposed to be. Like you said, you're both almost thirty years old. There's no excuse for his behavior."

"Let's change the subject. I don't even like to mention his name." She took a sip of her drink and then smiled brightly. "So, when is this move taking place?"

I blushed before answering.

"You already started, didn't you?"

"Well, we already spend most of our nights together. It just seemed easier to go ahead and start."

"I envy you," Becs' soft voice held the note of envy too. "The things you went through to get to this point suck, don't get me wrong. I just want what you seem to have with Houston, you know? That sweet, easy kind of love where you bond and just know that you are each other's forever?"

Her wistfulness matched my own whenever I thought about my relationship to Houston, especially in comparison to what Jeff and I used to have. There really was no good comparison where Jeff was concerned, which told me that I stayed in that relationship probably five years longer than I should have.

"I'm sure there will be trying times ahead, especially if our exes can't keep themselves away, but the difference is that we talk about everything. If one of us has a question or concern, instead of burying it, we just drop it right on the other person and work through it. I always thought I would hate a relationship like that, but it is so refreshing because there's never the fear of the unknown."

"I hate you a little bit right now, but then I get mad at myself for those feelings because you deserve that kind of happiness, Clea. I'm genuinely happy for you."

"Once my little niece or nephew is born, you're going to get back out there and find your person too." I shrugged then. "Maybe it'll happen sooner and they'll fall in love with you while you're growing this beautiful human."

"No way. I am not looking for love while I'm pregnant."

"Isn't that when Granna always says you find love?" I asked.

"What? When you're pregnant?" Becs teased.

"No, when you're not looking, it finds you."

"Pfft," She made the noise while sticking her tongue out at me. "I'm beginning to think that love just isn't in the cards for me. I'll be happy just raising my baby."

"And when your baby is grown and moves away?"

Becs shrugged. "I'll adopt a litter of puppies and raise them to be my sled dogs and we'll zoom off into the wild together."

"Wow, from paranoid to delusional in less than an hour. Maybe we should get your hormones checked out?"

Becs laughed at me. "It's my fantasy, don't spoil it."

"It's a lonely fantasy," I argued.

"Not really. You didn't let me get to the part where the were-bear of the wilderness stumbles upon me when my poor sled pops a skid. He saves, then ravages, me before taking my pups and I back to his lair which happens to be an amazing 5-star ski chalet for the world's elite."

"Holy shit, Becs, you need to stop reading so much romance! With those standards, you'll never find your one."

"I already found my one, Clea. He turned out to be a big disappointment though. I want to blame Jordan, but I can't. Every time I try, I just keep thinking, she had him basically her whole life. Why wouldn't she do whatever it took to hang onto that, especially when she thought the inevitable was promised?"

"Let me clear that up for you. If she had to wait for that inevitability just to win him, then he wasn't a prize worth winning and she'll be sorely disappointed when she finally realizes how much time she wasted and how many missed opportunities along the way too."

"I guess you're right."

"Of course, I am. I'm always right." I glanced down at my phone when it dinged.

> Houston: Did she agree to move into your place? I have Dallas and a couple friends on standby for tomorrow.

"Becs?"

"Yeah?'

"How does tomorrow sound for moving day?"

"Don't worry, Houston has some guys ready to take care of everything for you so you don't have to lift a finger."

Becs stood up immediately. "Oh my God! I have to go box up my bedroom. No way will a bunch of Houston's friends be boxing up my battery operated boyfriend or my panties for me." She leaned down and kissed my cheek. "See you tomorrow. And thanks for this, Clea. It means a lot."

"You never have to thank me," I told her before glancing down to respond to Houston as my friend saw herself out.

Clea: She's going to box up her unmentionables right now so that no one else sees them.

Houston: Good to know. Dallas will be disappointed.

Clea: Ewwww

AFTER GETTING Becs settled in at my house, Houston and I finally managed to sit down to eat a meal together. Granted, it was takeout and we were eating it on his couch. We were together at the end of the day though, and that was what mattered the most.

"If you want to change the furniture up, get new stuff, I'll understand." Houston was looking around at his furnishings as if seeing them for the first time. They weren't bad. He had a basic brown leather sofa and two matching reclining chairs. They were buttery soft leather, not the hard kind that is unforgiving when you sit on it. The only thing his place needed were little pops of color and a bit of a feminine touch.

"I like what you have."

"Are you sure?"

"Positive."

"Okay, you know you can do whatever you want with the place, it's yours now too."

"I'd rather do whatever we agreed to, than try to take over your space completely. So, let's just settle in and eventually we'll find things we want to add that will make this home ours and not just yours or mine."

"Every time I think it isn't possible to love you any more, you go and say something that changes my mind." Houston pulled me to him so that my legs had to straddle his and my core ground against his erection. "Kinda want to skip dinner and go straight to dessert."

"Yeah, we should definitely do that," I agreed heartily before his mouth descended to mine and swept me up in a blazing hot kiss that ignited my insides too.

My hips swiveled just enough to get his cock lined up with the needy parts of me so that the friction of our dry humping session would go a little further. Houston had other thoughts when I moved though and put his arm around my waist, and the other around my upper shoulders and neck, in an attempt to move us so that I would be underneath him on the couch.

Unfortunately, he tripped on the takeout bag that we let drift to the floor earlier when we emptied it of its yummy contents and I came down on the edge of the couch. Houston promptly let go of me to use that hand to brace for the fall, thinking that I wasn't as precariously perched as I was. The result was an awkward tangle of limbs, bump of heads, and a split lip from where my tooth banged into Houston's shoulder, only that stupid lip of mine was in the way and took the brunt of the force. We ended with my back braced against the bottom of the couch, Houston spread half on top of me and half on the floor to my side.

Our eyes met and we both burst out laughing.

That lasted just long enough for Houston to see that my

mouth was bleeding, at which point, he jumped up and panicked a little.

"Dammit, Clea! Why didn't you tell me you were hurt?"

"There really wasn't time to say anything in between it happening and us laughing over the ridiculousness," I tried to tell him, though some of it came out garbled since my lip had begun to swell a bit. Plus the blood. It was all I could taste in my mouth, which was a shame because it erased the kiss that started this whole thing.

"I'm grabbing some ice. Meet me in the bathroom," he ordered after getting me to my feet too. He ran off to the kitchen and called back over his shoulder. "Shit! I didn't check. Are there any other injuries you're hiding?"

He was completely serious, but my response was laughter. I loved the man. Loved that he didn't know quite what to do with his emotions in the wake of me being hurt. Sometimes, it was good to be cared for.

I got to the bathroom at the same time Houston rounded the corner with the bag of ice in hand. He started to give the ice to me, then paused. "Let me see first. You might need stitches."

I shook my head, but he wasn't having it. Instead, the infuriating man gently pulled my lower lip down and took a look at the tiny little slice on the inside of my lip that just happened to appear to bleed more profusely than it was. I'd venture to guess that all the spit in my mouth, thanks to the blood, was making it look more of a mess than it actually was. He dabbed the inside with a little gauze to get a better look and came to the same conclusion.

"I don't think it needs stitches, but you do need the ice because it's already getting puffy."

I rolled my eyes and applied the ice. Of course I would come out of tonight, our first where we were truly, officially living together with a fat lip. And a sore hip, but I wasn't going to tell him that part. He was worried enough.

Houston offered me a sympathetic gaze before speaking again. "It really is a desperate way to get out of a blowjob tonight, honey." Deadpan. The man's mouth didn't even twitch in humor until my jaw dropped, rather painfully, and he started laughing. I joined in for a brief moment before the movement pulled at my lip again.

"Ow! Ow! Ow!" I smacked his shoulder. "You jerk! Stop making me laugh."

Houston's arms flew around me and pulled us tight, so that I was enveloped in the comfort of his embrace. "Sorry you got hurt. In all seriousness, I will have to make up for your pain somehow. I suggest you get naked and go crawl in our bed and wait for me your legs spread. I'm going to clean up the mess in the living room and then come eat my dessert. You can have yours once you heal up." The sexy man winked and walked away from me then without waiting for a response. So, you know what I did?

You're damn right! I ran to our bedroom, got naked, and waited for his mouth to come take all my pain away. Best official move-in day ever!

14

"WHAT IN THE HELL IS HE DOING HERE?" I ASKED THE UNIVERSE AS Houston, and I pulled up to my old house to pick up Becs for her appointment.

"Tell me that's not your ex?" Houston growled angrily.

"I would, but then I'd be lying to you and I'm pretty sure we have a rule against doing that."

Houston grinned at me. "You will always make your jeans look good, baby." He winked. "Except that one time, with those unlucky jeans."

"Why would you bring that up right now? Seriously, Houston? My ex is standing there staring at us and you think it's a good time to talk about the night I shit myself in front of you?"

Houston chuckled away the distance between my lips and his and then he kissed me like I was his whole world. When he pulled away, I was in a Houston love fog and forgot where we were and why we happened to be there until Jeff started shouting us down from the top of his lungs.

"Really mature, Clea! I don't need to see you sucking face with another man."

I turned and jumped out of the car, angry beyond words. But boy-oh-boy did I have words to spare anyway.

"Are you fucking kidding me right now? You don't need to see me – the woman who is nothing to you but an ex – sucking face with her fiancé?" I laughed and cut him off before he could get a word in edgewise. "I walked in on you nailing my pregnant assistant to my desk at work in my office. You know what I didn't need to see? ANY OF THAT. I wish I could scrub it from my brain. But even if I could, then there would still be the laundry list of women that you have crawling out of every gutter in town with a claim to your dick and a baby in their belly. And all of them pre-date our breakup."

"Clea," Houston's voice rumbled in my ear as his front met my back and his arm twined around my waist to hold me protectively. "Why don't you go check on Becs and see if she's ready? I'll handle the trash."

I half-turned in his arms so that I could place a quick kiss on his all-too smoochable lips and then I jogged past Jeff, who just stood there stunned stupid. I wasn't really sure what was confusing to him though.

There was no way that I was missing the action, so I joined Becs at the front window and opened it a little further so the acoustics wouldn't be messed up and dilute what the two men had to say to one another.

"Fiancé?" Jeff asked Houston, obviously still gobsmacked over that revelation.

"Clea doesn't stutter," Houston answered my ex. "Neither do I. This is not the first time you've approached my woman since you were dumb enough to lose her, but it will be the last."

"Or fucking what, big man? You think I'm afraid of you in your little pansy-boy suits and ties? I'm not. Clea is pissed right now because I had a little case of cold feet, but that's it."

"Clea moved on the minute you proved you weren't the man she needed."

"Or a man at all," Becs called out helpfully from our perch in the window. The twitch in Houston's shoulders told me he was trying not to laugh at her.

"Clea just doesn't know what's best for her."

"And a man who cheated repeatedly, is known to have the dirtiest cock in town, and with a few babies on the way is what she deserves?" Houston asked.

"What the fuck did you just say about me?" Jeff bowed up and moved a couple steps closer to Houston with his fingers clenched into tight fists. Of course, Jeff being Jeff, he was doing it wrong and had his thumbs tucked.

"That's gonna hurt," Becs whispered to me.

I nodded, and then thought better of it.

"Think we should tell him?" Becs whispered again.

I shook my head. "It won't matter. He'll never get close enough to land a punch. If he breaks his thumbs on the air he hits, then wow. Just wow." We both giggled, then quieted down because I just wanted to enjoy the showdown. Jeff was an idiot. Why it took me so many years to see that was beyond my reasoning. I like to think I grew up at some point during that time.

"I'm just repeating what the rest of the town is saying about you. The ones who care about you enough to say anything at all, anyway." He smirked at Jeff. "Oh, and guess what? Clea isn't one of them because she doesn't think of you at all. Not until you show up and remind her of past mistakes."

"That's not fucking true," Jeff yelled at my man, and I felt a little bad for Houston, because I was pretty sure Jeff wasn't just saying it, he was definitely spraying it a little too.

"Yuck," Becs murmured, clearly having seen what I did.

"I'll fucking kill you!" Jeff yelled and that time, he swung wide, intending to... Becs and I both cocked our heads to the side to see what the hell Jeff had intended to hit since he threw his punch so wide that it actually threw him off balance and didn't come anywhere near making contact with Houston.

"Sorry, I think I might have twitched a little. Do you need to do a retake? I could try standing still. I mean, even more still than I was before when I twitched." Houston taunted him.

"Fuck you!" Jeff spun and lunged for Houston again, only that time, my beautiful man did not stand still. Instead, he grabbed Jeff's shoulder and head, yanked the idiot down until his face connected with Houston's knee and then he basically pushed him off like he was brushing a piece of lint from his suit.

"Pick yourself up. Get out of here. Don't bother Clea again. If I find out you've been sitting on this house one more time, I won't even bother with you. I'll send my brother Austin because being here means you're messing with the well-being of someone who belongs to him."

"What's that supposed to mean?" Becs whispered to me.

I grinned and shushed her. She'd figure it out eventually. I still had hope for Austin and Becs to realize they were meant to be together, if only Austin hadn't had baggage in the form of an obsessive best friend to contend with.

"This isn't over," Jeff yelled at Houston as he backed away with blood dripping down his obviously broken nose.

"I'm standing still again, asshole. If you're still feeling froggy, come play!" Houston held his arms out to his sides, palms up, as if he was waiting on the rapture to take him. Jeff glared at him, the window where he knew we were watching, and then back to Houston.

"She's not worth it," Jeff spat out along with a mouth full of blood.

"That's where you're wrong. You know you're wrong too, which is why you stupidly showed up here today. What you need to understand, Jeff, is that you are the part of the equation that is worthless. Clea is done with you. She's too good for you. She's always been too good for you. You fucked that up all on your own. Now, get the fuck out of here, go deal with your own shit, and don't come back.

15

"I'M SO THANKFUL THAT'S OVER WITH." I THREW MY SHOES OFF AND stretched my sore toes out.

Houston came in with a glass of wine in one hand and a beer in the other. "Pick your poison," he ordered.

"Well, it depends," I told him as I eyed the wine suspiciously.

"Is that something that actually tastes good, or stuff that pretentious people like to pretend tastes good so that they can impress all their other pretentious friends?"

Houston laughed. "It might as well be served in a juice box, totally Clea approved."

"Ah, perfect then I'll still take the beer because I don't need the wine headache tonight. I have plans for my mouth and the bottle will be a perfect warm up."

"Fuck!" Houston hissed through his teeth as he set both down on the counter beside him. The man stalked toward me, dipped his shoulder into my middle and ran for the bedroom with me draped over him like that.

I giggled and smacked his ass from my upside down vantage point. "Faster horsey! This is not the ride I ordered."

A stinging slap met my own ass then. "Behave, or I'll have to turn you over my knee and show you who is in charge."

"Mmm," I moaned before I leaned in and tried to bite his butt. Unfortunately I missed and ended up nibbling somewhere further up his back, but he still groaned deep and low and the noise set my womanly parts ablaze. I loved when my man couldn't help himself. When he was at my mercy, I was at my hottest.

Houston gently set me on my feet and started stripping off my clothes. "I just told you that I had plans for what was going in my mouth tonight. Generally, that means you need to be the one stripping, not me."

"But I enjoy stripping you down. Consider this pre-gaming." He leaned in and stole a kiss before nipping along my jawline and then tugging at my earlobe with is teeth. That sensation coupled with his warm breath and the scent that belonged totally to my man nearly put me in a sex haze I couldn't see my way out of. Honestly, I didn't want to see my way out of it either. Then again, I owed my fiancé for the manly display of valor he put on earlier that day in my defense. The fact that he didn't even have to try to defend me didn't matter. His willingness to do and the things he said, those were more than enough to earn him some rewards.

That was why I pushed Houston away from my very naked body. "Get undressed, I'll be right back!"

"What? Where are you going?"

"I promise, you'll like it. Just be undressed and ready for me when I get back."

"Not gonna argue with that," he said and his clothes were flying off at an alarming rate that made me put some pep in my step, lest I be a little late getting back to him.

Once I got to the kitchen, I opened the fridge and grabbed the bottle that I needed. I glanced at it and the fact that it was really cold and wondered for a minute if I needed to heat it up first.

"Nah, that shouldn't matter," I mumbled to myself as I ran

back to the bedroom with ass and boobs jiggling like gelatin all the way. "It doesn't matter if he doesn't see it," I reminded myself.

"If I don't see what?" Houston asked. I glanced up to find my gorgeous man totally naked, lounging across the bed with his cock proudly waving at me.

"What? Nothing."

"Whatcha got there, Clea?"

"Um, I just thought, well, you see, your brother had like one good idea in his whole life. But really bad execution of that idea," I rambled on.

"Why are we naked and talking about my brother?"

"Shit!" I jump-skip-ran to the bed in my haste to quickly replace my brother talk while naked with what I meant to try tonight. I had never played around with food, having heard horror stories in college about raging yeast infections after one of the girls who lived two doors down from us had an unfortunate incident with her boyfriend and a popsicle. It was not sugar free and it showed.

I glanced quickly down at the label on the bottle I held. Not sugar free either. Okay, one chocolate blowjob and then a shower before the rest of our sexy times. That was doable.

"Clea?" Houston asked, humor in his voice, but a little snap of impatience as well.

"Close your eyes."

"Clea?" He growled, but to my surprise, listened as well.

"I promise this will be really good, baby."

"Mmm," Houston moaned. "I like the sound of that."

I crawled across the bed and straddled his thighs, closer to his knees so that I would have room to bend and work. I wondered if that was going to be the best position, considering I would be locking his legs together, but decided it had to be this way to minimize the mess.

I popped the top on the bottle in my hands, turned it upside down and squeezed.

"Holy fucking shit what is that?" Houston yelped as he jumped up in shock. Unfortunately, because of the way I was positioned, when he jumped, his knee kicked me in the cooter and I rolled off of him in a huff of pain.

"Shit! Clea! I'm so sorry. Are you hurt?" I glared as he glanced down at his dick in horror, clearly not really concerned about how a knee-punt to my pussy might feel when his dick looked like it had been dipped in shit.

"What the fuck?" He asked again before he saw the bottle of chocolate sauce lying on the bed, dripping all over the comforter and then the asshole threw his head back and laughed so hard and so loud a toot popped out.

He straightened his back, and glanced at me guiltily. "It slipped," he said and then devolved into laughter again as I rolled around on the bed holding my poor, abused lady parts.

"Babe," he called out, but I chose to ignore him.

"Sweet, sweet Clea, I can guarantee you that Dallas did not hand over a bottle of Hershey's straight from the cooler. That stuff has to be room temperature."

"Well, how the hell was I supposed to know?" I yelled at him as he continued to laugh and pick up the bottle where he put it down on the nightstand. "All I know about food and sex is that it's messy and you know Giselle had a whole popsicle shoved up her twat as foreplay, so I didn't think cold mattered."

That wasn't entirely truthful, but he didn't need to know I contemplated heating the stuff up for like a nanosecond before I let my excitement to try something new get the best of me.

"Let me see," Houston said as he pulled my hands away from my pussy and splayed my legs open.

"Ow!"

His face scrunched up a bit. "Ouch. Nailed you pretty good there, huh?"

"Not really in the good way, Houston."

He chuckled. "Want me to kiss it and make it better?"

"I don't really think that's going to work."

"Okay, well," he glanced at the chocolate sauce that transferred from his dick to his hand and licked it off seductively. "Seems like the perfect time to try anal since I'm already messy."

"Ew! You are so fucking gross." I yelled at him as he rolled off the bed from laughing so hard.

"Your face was priceless though," he managed to get out through his stupid laughter. I only laughed inside because I couldn't let him know how charming I found him even when he was being crude.

"Come on," he offered me his hand. "Let's get cleaned up, we'll ice your pussy down, and drink that Kool-Aid shit you call wine for a while. Later, when we've forgotten all about this mess, you can give me that blowjob you promised."

"I might need the whole bottle of wine and then some to forget about this, babe. I should have known this would never go right. Your damn brother strikes again! I bet he's out there somewhere wearing that fucking diaper right now."

"As long as he has the bow and arrows on with it because I don't want to think about the fetishes Dallas might be into."

It was my turn to scrunch up my face in disgust again. "Yeah, I'm gonna need extra time to scrub that image off in the shower." I shivered as we made our way there and Houston went about cleaning up the mess I made.

Once we were all washed up and rinsed off Houston turned me in the shower to face him and then gently pushed down on my shoulders. I grinned at the eager little eyebrow wobble he did.

"I guess I owe you for helping with the mess I made."

"We'll get some bedroom-ready things to play with for the next time you want to surprise me, that way no one gets injured."

"Or toots unexpectedly," I threw in because fuck it, if I had to be slightly humiliated he wasn't living down his part in this either.

He smacked my ass and pushed again until I was on my knees.

"It's safe to be down here, right?" I joked. In response he fisted my hair tight and tugged until our eyes met.

"Clea, enough fun and games. Time to get down to business."

"Yes, sir."

"Now there's a game we can still play."

"Wfffs aa" I managed to get out around his dick.

"What's that?" Houston asked.

I rolled my eyes in response because I still had his dick in my mouth and that was exactly what I'd said. He chuckled and then groaned as I gave an overachieving suck on his cock in conjunction with a little rough tug on his balls.

"Fuuuck! Clea, what was that?"

Apparently my man had never had it a little rough down under and he seemed to like it a whole lot. I scraped my nails across his balls and tickled at his taint while sucking him down and humming.

"Clea, I'm about to embarrass myself for a whole different reason," Houston mumbled as I continued to assault his senses.

I used my spit to lube up a finger while continuing to suck him for all I was worth and then, I wiggled it around his backdoor. After his initial jump of surprise – which thankfully was nothing like the one I earned from pouring refrigerator cold chocolate sauce on his cock – he assumed that was as far as I would take it, but instead, I drilled my finger home slowly until I could tickle his prostate and he shot off like a rocket into the back of my throat.

The animalistic groan that he let out along with the nearly painful way he clenched my hair in his fist was enough to nearly make me climax too. I guess we both liked a little bit of rough play. I never thought someone tugging my hair like that would be a turn on, but oh was it ever!

"Get up here," my fiancé growled at me and acquiesced to his demand immediately. "We'll talk about getting permission to do that later, but right now, I need to check and see if your pussy is all better."

Houston moved us both out of the spray of water, turned it all off, and then tossed me on the end of the bed after removing the chocolate-covered comforter. "Looks like you're ready for me to kiss it all better after all. So pretty and wet for me. Was it sucking my cock that got you this bothered or was it when I yanked your hair?" He grabbed my length up in his fists and mimicked the move, with only a slightly lighter grip. My eyes blazed at him, and my pussy grew wetter.

"Yeah, you like that, huh?" He flipped me over, smacked my ass, then lined up right behind me and slowly pushed his cock inside me until his balls were sitting right against my clit. "I'm gonna get pierced down there," he growled as he pulled out and slammed back in. "So every time my balls slap into your little clit, you're going to feel it even more."

"Yes! God, Houston, yes!"

He used my hair to pull my body up so that my back came in contact with his chest. Then he reached around and tugged on my nipple. I moaned as the pleasure rippled through my body. "You gonna get these pierced for me too?"

"After we have babies," I suggested in my fuck-drunk state, not realizing what I'd just said.

Houston's response was immediate though. He pushed me back down, face first into the bed, grabbed my hips and started thrusting so hard I knew I'd feel this fuck-session for days. His fingers dug into my hip on one side and thigh on the other as he all but lifted me to meet each downward motion that had him bottoming out inside me and his balls slapping eagerly against my clit.

"You want me to fill you up with my babies first? Wanna make us a family, Clea?"

"Oh God!" I suddenly realized what he was saying, what I had said, but there was no stopping this train. I wasn't even sure I'd want to get off the ride if we could stop it. Instead, I surrendered completely. Who cared if it was slightly insane to make a family with someone who I hadn't been dating that long. Houston and I were solid. We were together. We had plans for our life. It would be okay.

"Take me, Houston. I'm yours forever."

"Even when I plant my babies inside you."

"Especially then."

"Good, get ready sweet Clea."

He reached underneath me and started pinching at my sensitive nipples once again and that, in combination with everything else, set me flying high into the land of orgasmic bliss.

LATER, while lying in bed cuddled up to my favorite big spoon, I managed to build up the courage to talk about the big things. "So, are we going to talk about any of that, or are we just chalking it up to in-the-moment sex talk?"

"Which part do we need to talk about?"

"Come on, handsome, the most important part," I teased and reached behind me to grab his balls gently. "Are you really going to get a piercing?"

"In the moment, I just kept thinking that if I had a piercing there it would up your pleasure so much."

"How do you know?"

My cuddly bear pulled me closer and snuggled his face into my neck. "You really don't want to know the answer to that."

I gasped. "Did you have a bi-sexual lover who had a piercing there?"

"What? No. Where do you come up with this shit?"

"Well you liked it when I," I stuck my finger in the air and mimed ramming it hard at something and then wiggled the tip just for fun. Houston tugged my hand down and trapped it in his hold between my breasts.

"There has never been a gay or bi lover in my life, not that there's anything wrong with it I just prefer pussy and at least a handful of tits to play with." I giggled because he actually grabbed a handful to make his point.

"So, how do you know then?"

"Is this really something you need to know or are you stalling on asking the more important questions?"

"Can't the answer be both?"

"You're a nut, Clea." He chuckled against my hair. "Dallas has one."

"Of course, he does. Hey, wait, I don't remember seeing any metal..."

Houston growled. "You shouldn't have been looking anyway, but if I recall correctly, my brother's cock was covered in chocolate sauce and some woman's mouth when you saw it, so chances are, you missed the metal."

"That's true." I huffed out a laugh because I loved getting my man all riled up.

"So, the other stuff?"

"Nipple piercings?" I asked, still trying to avoid the question. I don't know why, but for some reason I thought he might think I was totally crazy if I said I want kids as soon as possible. Most couples just wanted to be a couple for a while first. Not me. It always irked me with Jeff that we seemed to be waiting forever for the engagement, the wedding, and even then he wanted to wait even longer to have kids. It was like he had to delay doing any of those things with me for some reason and I worried that Houston would feel the same way. What Jeff did shouldn't affect me, but it did. It made me wonder what was wrong with me that he never wanted to start a family, but he never thought to be cautious with other women.

"You already told me your answer about those. Now, how

about we discuss the two of us having kids sooner rather than later."

"Yeah, about that. Remember when we thought I might be pregnant when that condom broke?"

"Of course, I do. It's when I asked you to marry me." He grinned down at me and kissed the top of my head. I snuggled deeper into his hold, loving the warmth he put off.

"Well, I was disappointed when Becs was the one who got the positive result and I didn't."

"Me too," Houston admitted.

"Seriously?"

"Yeah, sweetheart. Part of me was hoping, from the moment I noticed the condom broke, that it would be the lucky shot, you know?"

"The lucky shot? What a romantic!" I teased to lighten the mood a bit. "I think I was more panicked initially, but the longer I had to think about it, the more it was what I wanted."

"So, we'll get married and start having kids right away. How many do you want?"

"Just like that?" I glanced back over my shoulder so that I could see his eyes when I asked. There was nothing but love looking back at me.

"Yeah, just like that."

"When you know, you know?" I asked.

His grin grew even wider. "My dad is a smart man. Best advice he ever gave me."

"I think so too."

"Good. Now, maybe we need to practice how to make a baby now, and people can wonder about our motives at our wedding."

"So scandalous!" I laughed. "I can't wait to marry you."

"I'm going to love you forever, Clea Mercer."

"I like the sound of that, Houston Mercer."

16

FOUR MONTHS LATER

"I'M REALLY NOT TOO SURE ABOUT THIS DRESS WITH THESE HEELS." I commented for probably the tenth time.

"Oh hush, you'll be fine."

"Says my knocked-up bestie who gets to wear flats."

Becs laughed at me. "Well, you're the one who wouldn't wait until I got my figure back to march down the aisle toward your lover man."

"I still don't know why you aren't the one marching down the aisle, considering." I pointed at her belly, but Becs just offered a grim smile in return.

"It wasn't an option," she all but whispered.

"I know he-"

Becs cut me off. "He asked, but you and I both know that it was done reluctantly. Let's face it, we dated years ago for a very short time." She pointed to her burgeoning belly. "This happened as a result of a one-night stand years after he ghosted me for something that wasn't even my fault and didn't directly concern us. I couldn't agree to marry him."

My heart ached for Becs. Her one-night stand with Austin meant so much more to her. She thought it was the beginning of

them together again until Jordan showed up and ruined everything. I still can't believe he just ghosted her instead of owning up
to whatever he needed to.

"He asked you to marry him," I reminded her.

"I know. I was there."

"Right, but I'm saying that he never asked Jordan to marry
him when he thought she was pregnant with his kid. Even when
he thought that's what was going on, the minute he found out
that *you* were pregnant, he asked *you* to marry him."

Becs contemplated that for a moment and then shrugged it
off. "Probably because it was already a given that they were
supposed to marry."

"So, what? He was going to have two wives?"

"Those people in Utah do it, why not?"

I laughed. "Those people in Utah? Really Becs?"

"Yeah, I'm not trying to be some sister wife and making charts
for who gets the asshole on which night. Plus, she would have
seniority and I'm not playing second fiddle next to crazy-town who
tried to fake a pregnancy when she doesn't even have a uterus."

My eyes grew wide, but Becs wasn't paying attention to my
face at all. Instead, she continued to ramble. "Can you imagine?
What if no one knew about her medical shit and she tried to cut
me open and steal my baby like in those Lifetime movies or
something?" Becs legitimately cringed and grabbed onto her baby
belly for dear life, as if there was a real threat in the room.

"I would never allow that to happen."

"Agh! Shit!" If my best friend could have jumped out of her
own skin at that point, she would have. Austin stood there
glaring at her.

"You think I'd ever let anything happen to harm you or our
baby?"

"You harmed me and you did it for her, so yeah."

"Son of a bitch!" He mumbled before turning to me. "This is

for you. A gift from your groom. Your something blue," he told me before stomping back out of the room.

"You could have said something," Becs whispered-hissed at me.

"I gave you the eyes."

"What? No you didn't. Your eyes always look wild. What am I supposed to do with that?" She pointed at my face, as if it was the problem. I glanced over my shoulder in the mirror to see that today I was a stunning bride. Becs' dress was a match to mine, the only difference was the shade we each wore. Oh, and her big baby bump. Mine wasn't noticeable yet.

"Here, let me put this on you," Becs offered. I turned around so she could clasp the necklace for me. It was a small sapphire stone in the shape of a heart surrounded by a halo of diamonds. It was gorgeous.

"There's something here for you as well," I told Becs. I opened the box, knowing full-well who it was from since he had given it to me earlier. "This is also your something blue."

I put a necklace around her neck that had an angel pendant. Her hands were spread out and holding a blue stone to represent the little boy she had in her belly.

"Thank you, this is beautiful. You didn't have to," Becs gushed as she swiped at a tear that fell.

"I didn't do it."

"Then who?" She asked, but when I simply looked at her, she attempted to take it off.

"Leave it. He's trying to make amends. Let him. For your peace of mind and the baby's."

"Yeah? What if he flakes on us after the baby comes?"

"Then we bury him where no one will ever find his corpse."

"I have a shovel," a gravelly voice called out from the door. Damn, apparently we were meant to be interrupted at all the wrong times.

"Hi, Daddy!" I called out to him before shuffling over in my stupid heels to give him a big hug.

"You ladies ready?"

"Yep."

"Let's go," Becs said and she lifted her dress up in her hands and marched her butt out to the doors where we would take the walk down the aisle. "Um," My best friend glanced back at me for a moment and then back toward the aisle we were about to walk down.

"Something wrong?" I asked, knowing what was waiting for her at the end.

"Either you made my baby daddy your Maid of Honor or he's standing in the wrong place."

Mr. Mercer, Houston and Austin's dad, pulled Becs in for a hug then. "Take a leap of faith and let me walk you down that aisle to a better future with my boy."

"But he…"

"Is your one, just like you're his. He messed up big time, and if he does it again, I'll bring my own damn shovel along to help with that body." He winked at her then offered his arm for my best friend.

Truth be told, Austin had already been working his way back into her heart, but theirs was a story for another day. My father offered me his arm, and together we marched to the man who was going to live out the rest of my happily ever after with me.

"Are you ready?" My father asked.

"I do."

"It's not time for that part yet, baby girl."

My nervous giggles could probably be heard all the way at the altar, and if Houston's wide grin was any kind of confirmation, they were.

Becs made it to Austin first, with Mr. Mercer giving her away. My best friend was already in tears, but she wasn't running, so I guess she was ready to give him his final chance.

The moment my father put my hand in Houston's to give me away to the other Mercer brother, I felt a sting on my backside and our guests started laughing. I turned to see Dallas standing there in the middle of the aisle, wearing a damn diaper and a bow tie with his bow and arrows out. My gaze dropped to my feet where a shiny red arrow rested, the one that had just hit me in the ass.

"Think I got it right this time!" He winked at me and then ran to the back to take a seat or maybe get some actual clothes on.

"I kind of hope that's on the video," I whispered to Houston.

"Me too, because he definitely got it right this time."

WHAT'S NEXT?

Ghosted by Texas
Loved for the Holidays #2
Anne Storm

Austin
Loyalty to a life-long friendship cost me everything!
I wasn't sure if Becs would ever allow me to atone for my
screwups, but I was going to use every trick in the book to earn
the only treat I ever wanted. Her!

Becs
My heart ached for the loss of the man I once loved.
It ached even more when I found out I was carrying his baby.
Finding out the reason he ghosted me... Made my heart hurt
worse.
He had been tricked.
Could I love a ghost?
There was only one way to find out.

This is book 2 in the Loved for the Holidays Series. The first book is Cupid Broke My Heart. While they can be read as standalone stories, you should read them in order for optimal enjoyment.

Here is a sneak peek at Ghosted by Texas!

Prologue

As I scanned the party for Clea, who was supposed to meet me there twenty minutes earlier, my eyes landed on the man of my dreams.

It felt as though I could melt right into the rich, warm depths of dark brown that stared right back at me. When his lips kicked up into a lazy half smile, I swear to all that is right in the world, I freaking swooned. My legs threatened to give out, my heart stuttered in my chest, and stupid palms started sweating for no good reason.

He stood at least a good eight inches above my much smaller frame and those broad shoulders that tapered down to his trim waist only made the size difference seem that much more – wow. Yeah, that was the right word for him. He was all kinds of wow. A leggy sorority girl, who was much closer to his height, leaned into his arm and whispered in his ear. All the while, he never took those mesmerizing eyes off mine.

"Austin!" I heard the woman whine as she slipped away from his body and stomped her prissy foot into the ground. She couldn't be less subtle if she yelled, "Pay attention to me, dammit!"

He did not pay her any mind, and instead, made his way over to me. Our eyes never wavered from one another's as he moved closer. The jeans he wore clung to his frame in all the right ways, not too tight, but not so baggy that you couldn't tell his thighs were shaped with sturdy muscles underneath. He had a golden star shaped badge clipped to the black belt that ran through the loops of his jeans. A black t-shirt adorned his torso and boy did I wish it hadn't. Why couldn't the man have worn a costume that meant he needed to go shirtless like some of the meatheads running around the party?

Still, happy birthday to me! I'd consider him a present that I had to unwrap, if given the chance.

"You looked like the best kind of trouble from across the room, so I had to come find out for myself."

Oh shit! As far as pickup lines went, that struck a nerve. It was a different approach than the usual, "Hey beautiful" or "Did you fall from heaven?" bullshit that I'd heard at parties during my years at university.

"Is that so?" I asked.

He laughed at my question instead of answering it, and then reached out to push gently on my button.

Oh! I was a fucking idiot.

Clea and I decided to go against the grain and not wear super slutty costumes, like ninety-nine-point-nine percent of the other women on campus. We went with a board games theme. She was the Game of Life, and I was Trouble, the board game with the big button in the middle that you had to push to make the die inside bounce. The same button that my mystery hunk was playing with.

I laughed along with him. "Honestly, my best friend was supposed to be the Game of Life, but she hasn't shown up yet. Would you believe that I forgot what costume I was wearing?"

He grinned down at me. "As bulky as this thing is, it's hard to believe."

"Well, your sheriff's costume had me stunned stupid for a minute, so there's that," I admitted shyly.

"U.S. Marshall. Sheriffs have to wear uniforms." He winked at me as he pointed to all the yummy goodness hidden behind his street clothes, not a uniform.

"What would I ever do without you to school me on the differences?"

"Maybe you should stick close, just in case you need help with anyone else's costumes."

"I don't think I noticed anyone else's." Holy fucking word vomit. My cheeks flushed with heat. I wasn't normally a shy person, but I also wasn't the bold type of woman who outwardly came on to a man so strongly. There was just something about him that tugged at this cord inside me, almost like we were meant to be attached. If he tugged, I moved closer. If I tugged, he would too. I didn't doubt that for a second.

"I'm Austin."

"As in Texas?" I asked.

"The very same," he chuckled as he admitted that, and it felt like there was a story behind Mr. Texas's name that embarrassed him a little bit.

"I'm Becs," I told him.

"I think I'll stick to Trouble for now, and we'll see where the night takes us."

Yep, it was a very happy birthday for me, indeed.

Chapter 1

Before

Mr. Texas was far from perfect. That didn't change the fact that he seemed perfectly suited for me.

"Are you sure you don't want to watch the," I swear, the man almost gagged while trying to say the word, "romance."

"I promise, that is the last thing that I want to watch with you right now. It sets women up with unrealistic expectations and bores men to death." I pushed a fly-away piece of my very expensive, yet slightly grown out, dirty-blond dye job out of my eyes. "Besides, there's nothing like an adrenaline-fueled, action-packed movie to build up to the exciting part of a date, right?" I asked him, as his tongue all but rolled out of his mouth in cartoon fashion.

"Can we just skip the movie and go get married?" He teased.

"Are you sure you don't want to watch the romantic comedy?" I retorted as his grin widened while I teased him. "That sounded like a cheesy line from one."

Austin – otherwise known as Mr. Texas – moved in closer and tucked the stray hairs of my too-long bangs behind my ears as he catalogued everything about me. "Is your hair normally darker?"

I nodded. "It was naturally blonde when I was younger, and gradually darkened until the only way it goes blonde now is with some chemical help and a lot of sunshine. I don't get out in the sun as much these days, so this is thanks to chemical help. I guess I need to go get it touched up again."

My cheeks heated with embarrassment as I realized he must have taken notice of the roots that had grown out just a tad too much, since I had to pay for books a few weeks ago when the semester started and couldn't get the touch-up I needed.

"It looks good as is, but I bet you look just as stunning when it's naturally dark."

The heat in my cheeks was for an entirely different reason as his compliment settled in. Most men I'd dated had preferred the lighter hair and seemed displeased if I allowed my darker roots to show. It was encouraging that Mr. Texas didn't feel the same.

"You know, normally I'm not a movie for a date kind of guy," he stated as his hand engulfed mine and he tugged to get me moving in the direction of the ticket line. "Since this is our third date, I figured we should do something different, though."

"It's weird because the movie date is so cliché, but I've never actually been on one."

"You've never been on a date to see a movie?" He sounded shocked by that admission.

"Nope. Never."

"Huh, well, we're about to change that and hopefully, it will be a night you'll never forget."

Austin was already well on his way to becoming a man I'd never forget. This was date number three, in less than two weeks. That was something unheard of for me. I was the date-around and never get serious girl. Sure, I wanted that romantic forever just as much as the next girl, but I'd never met someone who would fit the bill of the leading man in my romantic story. That changed when Mr. Texas came breezing into my life at the Halloween party I'd gone to on my birthday.

There was no way I could say no to a man who had seen me through that horrendous costume while surrounded by scantily clad angels, demons, and pirate wenches. It was weird to think that had been two weeks ago, because it felt like I'd known him forever. I wanted to punch myself in the mouth for feeling that way, because it wasn't normal and felt more like one of those unrealistic romantic comedy movies I'd just avoided. I loved those movies when I was with my bestie, Clea, watching them. They wouldn't do for a date though because I would compare what was going on with Austin to them.

Kind of like what I was already doing in my head.

"Do you want popcorn and a drink or something else?" Austin asked as we approached the counter.

"Can people watch a movie without the obligatory popcorn and soda?"

That grin that I couldn't get enough of popped to full effect as he turned to order a large tub of buttered popcorn and two drinks. "Reese's Pieces too, please."

"Sure," he agreed easily. "Can you add a box of the Reese's

Pieces?" He asked the girl working the counter who tripped over her own feet because she was too busy staring at Austin to function properly. Me too, girl. Me too.

"You're not allergic to peanut butter or anything, are you?" I asked as an afterthought.

"Nope."

"Good. Do you mind if we dump the candy into the bucket of popcorn?"

"Seriously?"

I nodded. "Trust me. It's the best thing ever."

"I'll try almost anything at least once," he answered, though the dubious look he threw at the box of candy said something entirely different.

"You won't hate it," I promised.

Once we took our seats, Austin hesitantly started to dump the candy into the popcorn. I took it from him, shook the bucket, then dumped some more and repeated the process a few times until the box of candy was empty.

"I see there's a system." He chuckled as he eyed the bucket in my hands. The answering grin and nod of my head confirmed.

"There needs to be equal displacement, otherwise it just all sits there on top and that's no fun. Half the experience is dipping your hand in for some popcorn, once the lights go low, and ending up with a mouthful of salty-sweet goodness instead."

Austin leaned in so quickly, it took me until his lips landed on mine to process the move. Once I did, I was already lost to his kiss as his tongue teased at the crease of my mouth until I opened and invited him to explore me further. He groaned and pulled away far too soon for my liking.

"That's more my kind of a salty-sweet surprise, since we're sharing the things that we love."

"I seem to be a fan, too." My voice sounded breathy and not at all like it usually did. I'd never had a kiss that took my breath away before.

As the lights dimmed, Austin reached over and took my hand in his. "I've never connected so easily with anyone else on this planet," he admitted. I turned to see him ducking his head, almost as if he was embarrassed by admitting something like that to me.

"I feel the same," I agreed. "I don't know why. Normally," I paused, hesitating to say the rest.

"Normally?" He prompted.

"When I date," I groaned in frustration with myself over what I was about to say. "I could take them or leave them and mostly, if I'm being honest, leave them. It's been about three years since I went out on a third date with anyone because they usually just feel lackluster in some way."

Austin leaned in and kissed me again as the pre-movie local commercials swapped to a preview of the latest super-hero blockbuster. As our lips parted, he smiled warmly at me. "You took the words right out of my mouth, Trouble."

It was probably a good thing that the lights were too low for him to make out the blush that stole across my cheeks in the wake of his agreement. I was stuck in my head, thinking about the tingly sensation left behind on my lips, when his groan of pleasure forced me to look his way again.

Austin's eyes were on mine as his jaw worked while he chewed. "You were right. Now, I wonder why I never thought to do this before."

"Do what?" I asked, still in a kiss-induced la-la-land.

"Add the Reese's Pieces to the popcorn. The hot popcorn kind of made it slightly melty, but the candy coating resisted the melt and held it all together until it got in my mouth. Mixed with the buttery popcorn, it's the best thing I've put in my mouth, next to your lips." He winked and grabbed another handful from the bucket.

Austin raised the arm of the theater seat that was between us and pulled me closer to him so that I ended up snuggled into his side for the duration of the movie as we munched, occasionally trash-talked a character, and just enjoyed being with one another. I never knew movie dates could be so damn perfect.

As we walked out of the movie theater, and into the parking lot while holding hands, Austin stiffened and looked nervously toward where we'd parked earlier. He spun me, so that my back was to the car, and I faced him. It was such a quick move, that I giggled, thinking he was trying to be romantic and steal another kiss.

I continued to think that, until I noticed that he was watching something, or someone, over my shoulder with what seemed like trepidation in his gaze and maybe a little guilt. The butterfly feeling in my gut moments ago, transferred into something heavier, souring the popcorn and candy I'd ingested during the movie.

"Is something wrong?" I asked Austin. His eyes came down to meet my own briefly before he sighed and shifted his gaze to stare at his feet. I took the opportunity to glance over my shoulder, where I found a woman standing there with a hurt look on her face. She wasn't so much standing as leaning on a car parked right behind Austin's. It was obvious, by the popcorn bag still in her hands, that she had just been in the theater to see a movie as well. The problem was, her sullen look shifted to a scornful one as her eyes left my date's and moved to take me in.

"Who is that?" I asked before turning my attention back to Austin.

"She's, fuck, it's hard to explain."

"It's really not, Austin. Who is she to you?"

"She's been my best friend ever since I could remember," was his answer. That wasn't so bad. Maybe he had blown her off to go on our date. If that was the case, I could understand her being angry with the situation. "We've grown into something more though," he admitted which completely burst the platonic bubble I'd been shaping around them.

"Something more?" I prompted, hoping he meant anything other than what it sounded like.

"We're not dating, serious or anything, Becs. It's not like that. It's just that when neither of us is seeing someone, we sometimes hook up, too."

"So, that's your fuck buddy over there giving me the evil eye?" I snipped at him.

"Don't say it like that. We've done nothing wrong," he insisted.

"It sure does feel like you're doing something wrong, considering the death glares that are heating up my backside," I argued.

"We're not like that. She has no right to be angry or jealous or whatever the hell is going on. We're friends," he tried to reiterate.

"You are friends who fuck. Didn't anyone ever tell you that you can't be fuck buddies with your best friend? It doesn't work like that. There are feelings involved."

"I promise, it isn't like that."

"Oh? Then you don't mind calling her over here to straighten that out while I'm able to hear her confirm?"

"What? No, that would just be cruel and awkward."

"Cruel to whom?"

"What do you mean?"

"If she's just a friend, then clarifying the fact that you are only friends, who happen to fuck when you're not seeing someone else, shouldn't be cruel to anyone. If you're lying, then I guess it would be cruel to both that woman and myself, Austin. I'm telling you now, either you call her over here and get this out in the open, or whatever we started between us ends here."

Austin stared at me for a moment, as if I might change my mind, and then his shoulders slumped and he took a step to the left and crooked his finger, inviting the woman to join us.

My stomach had gone from being filled with beautiful butterflies to lead balloons, and now it felt like a bottomless pit about to suck me into a hellscape of my own making. Why had I thought confronting the other woman in Austin's life was a good idea? Shoot. Wait. Was I the other woman? He was dating me, but they were lifelong friends and fuck buddies for who knew how long. Dammit, logistically, that made me the other woman.

My cheeks flushed with embarrassment at the thought as I turned to greet the naturally blonde girl who stood only a few feet behind us.

"What's going on, Aus?"

"Jordan, this is Becs," he introduced *her* to *me*. That didn't sit well because I was his date for the night. It felt like that introduction should have gone the other way.

"And?" She turned that one word into an effective question with the attitude that dripped from it. If I thought she resented me spending time with Austin, it was proven by how she responded.

"And, since you're throwing around so much attitude, my date had questions about our relationship," he added.

Jordan glared my way before turning her attention back to Austin and smiling viciously. "Did you tell her we were best friends?" She asked, to which Austin nodded his head, and I could almost see the relief alleviate some of the sag that weighed his shoulders down. His bestie wasn't quite done, though. "Or that we fuck? A lot," she tacked on those last two words before turning her venomous smirk back my way.

"Why are you being like this?" My date asked the woman. "I told her that we had an arrangement whenever we weren't seeing anyone else."

"Yeah? Well considering we exercised our arrangement just a few days ago, and had plans tonight that got cancelled unexpectedly, I wasn't aware that our arrangement was paused again."

A few days ago? That lead balloon feeling morphed to something far worse as I felt the need to hurl my popcorn and candy mixture.

"It's been weeks, not days," Austin corrected as he huffed out a frustrated breath. The woman grimaced and shrugged her shoulders, as if that little fact changed anything. It did, in a way. At least he hadn't been having sex with her while he was trying to date me. That would have been a lot worse.

"I wasn't aware there was any arrangement with another person before five minutes ago," I explained to the woman. "I'm sorry for that because I never would have gone out with him had I known."

Jordan ducked her head, seeming almost embarrassed by my admission. Austin turned on a dime and reached out to take hold of my arm and stop me from moving any further away from him.

"Becs?" He questioned with a hint of desperation in his voice. "Please, stop. I don't want you to leave. It's not like I've been seeing you both at the same time. I haven't even seen Jordan since last week, and that was only in the gym on campus. I haven't been with her since before the day I ran into you."

Jordan sucked in a breath, no doubt realizing that he cut her off, apparently without a conversation about it, the day he met me.

"It looks like you have some things to work out with your *friend*. That was something you should have done before asking me out," I scolded him. "This is an awkward position for me because you made me the unknowing other woman. You should have clarified a bit better when I asked if you were dating anyone."

Austin cut me off, but that was all I had to say to him. "I told you that I wasn't seeing anyone, and that was the truth."

I scoffed. "That was your cue to come clean about having a regular fuck buddy. Don't try to bullshit me with semantics, Austin."

"It's the truth, though. I never would have touched Jordan again while dating you."

"But the minute we end things, you'll be right back in her bed, right?" I asked, hurt on Jordan's behalf that he could so callously dump her and then expect to pick right back up when she was convenient again. He shrugged sheepishly and I turned to look at the woman whose cheeks were flaming with embarrassment.

"We've only ever been friends who have sex when we're both single," she admitted while kicking at a pebble that seemed to be taking all her concentration.

"When was the last time you were the unavailable person in your little arrangement?" I asked out of curiosity. The woman glanced up at me, a pained expression in her eyes, and I knew the answer without her having to say a word. She hadn't been dating other people. Jordan was waiting for Austin to take their relationship seriously and become more than a fuck buddy or his friend.

"I can't do this," I told Austin, before turning and getting the hell out of there as quickly as possible. I ignored Mr. Texas as he pleaded for me to come back. There was no way in hell that would ever happen. It was a damn shame too because there was a spark with Austin that I'd never experienced with another man in all my years of dating. We clicked on this crazy, other-worldly level that I dared to call magical when I told my best friend about him. Unfortunately, the magic turned out to be a healthy dose of deception and disappointment.

ALSO BY ANNE STORM

Loved for the Holidays Series

Cupid Broke my Heart

Ghosted by Texas

Resolving Rumors

Cheating Hearts Series

The Homewrecker's Fate

The Regrettable Mistake

Savage Vipers MC Series

Wait for Me

Devastate Me

Surprise Me

Baby Me

∽ℐ

ALSO BY CHRISTINE MICHELLE

Standalone Romances

Bad at Love

His Bittersweet Regret

Letters to Lily

The Groupie Journal

Winter Wolves (PNR)

The Fortunate Ones

Robeson Family Novels Series

The Forgotten Wife

When the Last Petal Falls

Aces High MC - Charleston Series

The Other Princess

A Love so Hard

The Princess and the Prospect

The Killing Ride

A Twist of Fate

Everlasting

A Year and a Day

The Broken Beginning - Part One

The Broken Beginning - Part Two

Aces High MC - Dakotas Series

Dancing with Danger

Whiskey Tango Foxtrot

The Restart and the Remedy

Aces High MC - Tallahassee Series

Crushed

Aces High MC - Cedar Falls Series

Redemption Weather

Smoke and the Flame

Proven

Aces High MC - Sierra High Series

Walker

Trouble

S.H.E. MC Series

Angel Girl

JoJo

Keys

Dark Leopards MC Series (PNR)

Ridden by Darkness

The B Team

T.I.E. (The Infinite Everything) Series

The Infinite Something

The Infinite Beat

Valhalla Rising Series

Revived

Mirage island Mates (PNR)

Into the Grasslands

Beyond the Grasslands

The Ancients Series (PNR)

Shadows of the Ancients

Falling into the White

Branches of the Willow

Bound by the Moon

Vukodlak Brew Series (PNR)

Entwined

Enraged

The Awakening Trilogy

Birthrights

Revelations

Incarnations

Death Viewers Series (Paranormal Suspense)

Breathless

Other Works (YA/NA Paranormal and Dystopian):

The Voodoo Follies

Catch a Falling Star

ABOUT THE AUTHOR

Anne Storm is a pen name for Christine Michelle.
Anne Storm's books:
Dark romance/subjects with triggers
Christine Michelle's books:
(mild) MC Romance, Rock Star Romance, paranormal romance
and suspense, and other Contemporary Romance
If you want to learn more about Christine, her books, or her
crazy adventures into the wilderness, you can find out more
through the following links:
Website & Newsletter sign up:
www.moonlitdreams.org
Signing up for the newsletter also gets you first option at future
Beta reading and ARC (advanced reader copy) giveaway
opportunities!
**Universal links to everything
(social media, book links, and more)**
https://linktr.ee/christinemichelle

facebook.com/M00nlitDreams
instagram.com/christinemichelle_annestorm
tiktok.com/@christine.michelle.books
bsky.app/profile/annestorm.bsky.social